FLIP CITY

FLIP CITY

SPRING HERMANN

Orchard Books
A division of Franklin Watts, Inc.
NEW YORK

ORCHARD BOOKS
387 Park Avenue South
New York, New York 10016

ORCHARD BOOKS CANADA
20 Torbay Road
Markham, Ontario 23P 1G6

Orchard Books is a division of Franklin Watts, Inc.

MANUFACTURED IN THE UNITED STATES OF AMERICA
Book design by Tere LoPrete

10   9   8   7   6   5   4   3   2   1

The text of this book is set in 12 pt. Caledonia

Library of Congress Cataloging-in-Publication Data

Hermann, Spring.
    Flip City.
        Summary: Four girls whose family lives are
difficult compete in gymnastics for their gym,
Flip City, the place where they feel most at home.
        [1. Gymnastics—Fiction.   2. Family problems—
Fiction]   I. Title.
PZ7.H43167Fl   1988   [Fic]   88-60096
ISBN 0-531-05785-2
ISBN 0-531-08385-3 (lib. bdg.)

ACKNOWLEDGMENTS

Special thanks for invaluable technical assistance to:
Kip Reed and Maureen Chagnon, gymnastic coaches;
formerly of Gymnastic Training Center,
now of New England Gymnastic Express,
Newington, Conn.

Thanks also for help from the following:

Steve Reige and his eighth-grade English class
Watkinson School, Hartford, Conn.

Arthur Querido, Counselor, and the staff of
Hartford Public High School, Hartford, Conn.

Yarislav Stremien,
Abby and Liat Hoffman,
Ahn Tho and Quynh Nguyen,
Tuyen Le and her family,

and especially
Amy, Ellen, and Laura Myerson

Contents

FLIP CITY

1
Heading for the Gym
September 5

Mercy Samuels stepped in front of her mirror and yanked up her sleeveless leotard. Sucking in her stomach, she studied her figure from all angles. No, there was no hope that her coaches would miss the ten added pounds. Disgusted, she pulled on baggy nylon shorts and her brother's extra large T-shirt stamped "Franklin High Athletic Dept." Not that she could disguise her problem. Eileen's X-ray vision would spot the gain as soon as she hit her first splits. And when Joe sent her to the uneven parallel bars, she'd try to push up and fail, or swing through with her legs piked for the "kip"—and fall flat on her behind. "First day back at Flip City after summer break," she thought, "and I'll look like a total loser."

As Mercy ran down the stairs to the kitchen, she suddenly felt dizzy and grabbed the banister. Too sick for workout? She grumbled, "Jerk, it's just nerves. That and no lunch."

Mercy grabbed an apple and a low-fat yogurt and ate quickly while skimming her assignment notebook. Eighth grade already was hard. Her American history teacher had mentioned several reports. When, she wondered, would she find time to sit at the library and do research? Workouts at Flip City, the gymnastic training center where she competed on the Class III team, kept her busy from four to seven every weekday except Wednesday. Saturdays, her team competed in meets with other gymnastic schools, many of which were several hours' drive away. Only Sundays remained for Mercy to go to church, see her friends, do chores, read homework assignments, and try to find time to relax. Still, in spite of her battles with weight and scheduling, Mercy couldn't wait to get to Flip City. She was definitely hooked.

A horn sounded, and Mercy galloped out to meet her mother. Dad's shift as a firearms factory foreman didn't end until five, and her older brothers had football practice until after six, but Mom got off at three-thirty from her job as secretary for an insurance company, so she drove Mercy to Flip City. Until now Dad or her brothers had made the return drive after seven. But this fall a new gymnast had moved to their neighborhood, and her father had offered to car pool.

"Hi Mom," Mercy said. "Remember we have to pick up Dina."

"Right, on Kane Street. So we can actually have a calm family dinner now, without Dad or Fred or Ernie dashing off." Alma Samuels gave her daughter an apologetic grin. "Wish you could join us."

"No big deal," Mercy shrugged. "I know Dad and the boys would be starving if they waited until seven-thirty." Mercy had eaten so many meals alone due to gymnastics that she accepted it. Fred and Ernie's afternoons were consumed by football practice; they raced home at six, ravenous. Football season ended by Christmas, whereas training season in a private gym school ran over nine months. Sometimes Mercy wished that on those dark cold winter nights when she came home whipped from workout they'd wait dinner for her—but they never did.

Now she would have a fellow gymnast to keep her company during the long commutes, someone who also felt that the joy of gym competition was worth all the sacrifices and solitary dinners. And if this Dina had at least a small poundage problem, so much the better.

Dina Dibella paced her front porch, pretending to watch her little sisters kick the soccer ball. "Dina, watch this pass!" her sister Rose kept shouting. Dina smiled, hiding the nerves churning her stomach. Her mom had made her eat a bowl of soup, which felt like lead in her stomach. Dina was eager to get back into training after a summer break, but she was fearful of being the odd one on a team where girls had known each other for years.

Dina's family had been living on Kane Street for only a month. Pop could have chosen to live in any of several towns in his new sales territory, but he had moved the family here because of the proximity to Flip City. So each day Dina walked alone to Schindler Junior High, confused and scared of getting lost, forgetting her locker combination, being late, or having the older boys tease her. Now as she watched the Samuelses' car head for her driveway, Dina grew panicky. First a new neighborhood, then an entire seventh grade full of unfamiliar faces, and now this: a gymnast called Marcie who'd expect her to make clever conversation! It didn't do any good to tell herself there was no reason to be so shy. Spending a half hour in the back seat with a strange girl was almost more than Dina could endure. What if she was shy too?

As the Samuelses' horn beeped, Dina grabbed her nylon tote bag, rushed past her sisters, who were wrestling on the lawn, and jumped in the car.

"Hi Dina," Mercy said as they drove off. "This is my mom."

"Yes. Hello. Uh, Marcie?"

"It's *Mercy*. Don't worry, everybody gets it wrong."

"Oh sure. Mercy."

"I know it's weird. My grandmother and her sisters got named for feminine virtues, since they were all Quakers. I got named for my grandma. Better than Aunt Chastity, right?"

"Right," Dina nodded, tight-lipped.

Mercy waited for Dina to grin in return, thinking, "Is this kid a little slow? No sense of humor? And she can't be going to Schindler. She looks like she's about ten." Then she said aloud, "So you just moved here from Albany? What did you compete there?"

"Well," Dina swallowed, "I did Class III. Compulsory routines, not optional. But I had a big problem with one event. Beam. So Pop decided I'd better do another year. In compulsory."

"Same with me," Mercy said, glad to hear that a girl with such an incredible body could also have weaknesses. "I really blow it on bars. Our Class III coaches are so hard, especially Joe. Eileen's not as tough as Joe, but she's picky. Joe coaches my best and worst: vault and bars."

"So who coaches the beam?" Dina asked. "Marion Rothman?" That was the name of the famous coach that Pop had mentioned.

"Eileen coaches beam. Marion's the big boss lady," Mercy explained. "She only coaches Class IIs and Is. Of course, she knows what each of us is doing. Joe and Eileen tell her everything. They say she just about lives at Flip City. Did you know she was on the U.S. Olympic Team, back in the sixties?"

Dina nodded. Pop had checked her out.

"My friends in Class II say she runs their buns off, and she keeps the Class Is working half the night. She's *so* tough."

Dina nodded again, trying hard to think up a clever response. She could hardly tell this person she had just met that Pop would be upset to hear Marion wasn't going to coach her. She ought to be in Class II this season anyway, except she kept choking and freezing and absolutely falling apart on the beam exercise. And when a gymnast was a real flop in one event, no matter how strong she was in the other three, the move up to the next class just could not be made.

"So when did you start doing gymnastics?" Mercy asked, wondering if Dina was snobbish about leaving a big-city gym and coming to little old Flip City. Maybe that was why she hardly talked and kept looking out the window?

"Uh, when I was ten. Kind of late. When my father . . . had the time to take me. I did a year in Class IV and last year in Class III."

"You must learn fast," Mercy said. "And you'll like Flip City. It's the greatest. Want to hear about some of the girls on our team?"

Dina nodded and managed a smile. Mercy was really nice, easy to get to know. As she listened to Mercy chat about Jules and Von, two girls she'd competed with for years, Dina relaxed slightly. Maybe Flip City really could become her new home.

Julia Katherine Wolcott sat at the immense stainless-steel table in her kitchen, wolfing down a huge tuna-Swiss-and-tomato sandwich and a chocolate milkshake. The housekeeper, Evalene, sat across from her, dividing her attention between the clock, the mini-TV on the counter playing *Guiding Light*, and Jules's progress with her "snack."

"Finish that, Little Jewel. We got to go, pick up Von. Don't want to be late, first day back?"

"Ummm." As she chewed, Jules studied her hands. After a summer away from the gym they were almost pretty, perfectly filed and polished nails capping her long bony fingers, and palms nearly free of callouses. "Get out the old Vitamin-E oil. Here I go back on the bars, where I'll rip up these hands for sure."

"Yeah, but you like bars. That's almost your best," Evalene said as she grabbed her Red Sox cap and Patriots jacket. "We get you tough again. Now let's go!" Jules swallowed the last bite as Evalene rushed her out the back door.

As Evalene headed the Buick toward the south end of the city, Jules fretted about her return to the gym after a summer spent lazing around her family's beach house. "I should have done a summer workout," she said. "You could have driven me up a few days a week. Now I'm going to be *so* bad."

"Your mother wanted you down there, Jewel," Evalene reminded her. "She say, you need more sun and rest. Spend time with other nice young ladies at the beach."

"Mother doesn't have to get up on those bars today," Jules grumbled. "And you know what? I tried on all my fall pants, and they're three inches too short. I'm going to need a whole bunch of new clothes."

"You be fourteen soon. Look at your father and grandfather, how long their legs. You going to come out like them."

Jules smiled at Evalene, the stocky Polish immigrant who had worked for the Wolcotts since Jules was born, the only housekeeper for the only child. Although the family had had a series of cleaning women and yard men, Evalene and Jules had always been together.

"I could get too tall for the bars," Jules stated. "My feet could drag."

"Why you worry?" Evalene said. "Those coaches, they fix the bars right for you." She drove rapidly, skimming the yellow lights. Soon they traveled the streets of the South End, past the Spanish Cantina, the pizzerias, the Portuguese bakery, the Saigon Café (run by Von's elder sisters). Silently Jules stewed about her sudden growth spurt. She did not understand the physical dynamics of why tall people, both male and

female, did not do well in gymnastics—she only knew
that smaller bodies mastered the skills more easily. It
was possible for Jules to outgrow the sport. If only she
could look like her friend Von, who, like all the mem-
bers of her family, was compact and muscular. Then
Jules could compete at Flip City forever, the place
where she felt strong, pretty, and confident.

In front of the Oriental Grocery and Gifts, Von Nguyen danced along the curb as if it were a balance beam,
skipping, turning, posing on her toes. As she danced,
she downed an ice cream cone. Petite, hipless, yet
powerful, Von prided herself on her balance and poise.
When she saw the Wolcotts' Buick, she shouted goodbye to her parents through the open door of the store,
then dashed into the avenue.

"Hi Jules, hi Evalene. Jules, you're still tan! Did
you have a terrific summer at the beach?"

"It was fine," Jules replied. "Kind of boring at the
end. What did you do, work in the store?"

"No, my sisters let me work in their café clearing
tables. It was much better than doing stock—I made
tips. Going to spend them all on cool clothes."

"Did you grow a lot too?" Jules asked.

"No, it's not that," Von said. "I'm at Bush now, and
you *have* to look cool."

After two weeks as a freshman at Horace Bushnell
High, Von had the message: she'd be lost if she didn't
look as if she fit in. Not many of her former classmates
from Saint Anne's School went on to Bushnell High;
most went to Loyola, a Catholic academy. Von should
have been there too; her parents wanted her there,

but the Nguyens couldn't afford two tuitions and Von had pleaded to stay in gymnastics. The city kids at Bush joined gangs for protection, groups centered on ethnic backgrounds, a sport, or a club. Von didn't want to depend only on the Vietnamese kids for her gang, and her sport was based at Flip City. The wrong clothes branded her as an outsider, a nerd freshie. She didn't smoke or use the right street talk. Twice she'd gotten roughed up in the bathroom. But Von was determined to find a good crowd, a mixed group, and survive.

When Jules asked, "How are you doing at Bush?" Von decided to keep the troubled parts of her life from her Flip City friend. "I'm doing O.K.," she said. "Learning my way around. It's big. But I'll make it." She then changed the subject: "Jules, your eyes look different."

"New tinted lenses. Do they look phony?"

"No." Von studied Jules's wide-set eyes. The dull hazel color now appeared to be a warm, flecked green. "They're excellent! Just use some green and brown shadow and liner to bring them out. How about your braces? All gone?"

"Finally," Jules sighed. "Except I have this retainer, which I think I have to wear until I get married."

"Yeah? Well, as long as you lose it on your honeymoon."

Both the girls giggled. Soon they glimpsed the sight they'd missed over the summer: down a bumpy road in an industrial park north of Hartford, a former warehouse gleamed white in the September sun, its huge rolling doors and grated windows painted a bright red, the large emblem over the entrance stating, FLIP CITY.

Mercy led Dina into the changing room, where gymnasts of various ages and sizes stripped down to leotards and T-shirts for workout. Mercy scanned the room for Jules and Von, not having heard for certain if they were returning to competition. Juggling finances was always a consideration for the Nguyen family, Mercy knew—and if Von had elected to go to Loyola Academy, then she wouldn't be back. But Von hadn't called Mercy to tell her the big decision, so Mercy had to wait with the rest of the team to see if Von, the Class III highest all-around scorer, would return. And although money was never a factor for Jules's family, Mercy sensed that the Wolcotts were getting sick of the gym taking up so much of Jules's time. They too might have called it quits on Flip City.

"There they are!" Mercy said to Dina. "The two kids I told you about. Hi Jules, hi Von!"

"Hi Mercy!" Von said. "Yeah, we're back. I decided to go to Bushnell High. How could I live without you guys?"

"And this gorgeous place?" Mercy added.

The girls inhaled grandly. Although the changing room was freshly painted, an aroma lingered.

"Eau de Sweat Sock," Mercy grinned.

"I love it!" Jules said. "Mother gags every time I walk in the house. And I'm only back here because Daddy stuck up for me, and I swore I'd improve my grades."

"O.K. guys," Mercy said to the group. "This is Dina

Dibella, and she's a Class III who just moved down from New York. She's at Schindler Junior High with me, but she's in seventh. This is Jules, and Von, and Loretta, and Amy . . ."

Mercy went down the team lineup. Dina nodded, smiling tensely. She'd stripped to a tight high-cut red leo, revealing one of the most smoothly-muscled, efficient five-foot bodies that Mercy had ever seen. Dina looked both more petite and tougher than Von. A wave of resentment hit Mercy—Dina would never fear a weigh-in. Life was definitely not fair.

Jules helped Dina get her names straight: "Jules is really Julia, but my housekeeper always calls me Little Jewel, so I got the nickname."

"Von is Vietnamese, but since we left when I was three, I don't remember much about it."

Loretta, Amy, and the four others in the nine-to-eleven age group smiled admiringly at Dina, whom they could see was more mature than they despite her size. "How old are you?" Loretta asked bluntly.

"I'll be thirteen at Christmas," Dina replied. She spoke quickly; nerves made her sound cool, clipped.

Mercy exchanged glances with Jules and Von, which said, Is this kid going to be a pain? "Come on, Dina," Mercy said. "I'll show you around." The girls filed into the main gym area with its high eye-beamed ceiling and large multi-paned windows. "I'm the tour guide because I've been here the longest—since fourth grade."

"That's right," Jules said. "I started in fifth, back in Class IV. And Von took gym in some small acrobatic school or something, didn't you, Von?"

"Yeah, but the teacher was a loser, so Mother let me start at Flip City in sixth grade. I learned so much here in one year, I couldn't believe it. Last year I did make it into Class III optional meets, but Joe said I needed another year's experience before I go into Class II."

"Look, Dina, up there." Mercy pointed to a former storage loft which had been remodeled into a viewer's gallery and glass-partitioned office. "That's Marion's Penthouse. You know, the Boss Lady." As Dina strained to see the great coach, Mercy assured her, "Marion's always up there, you just can't see her when she's bent over her desk. But she can see *you*."

"Yeah, she's got a periscope," Von teased Dina.

"And here's the equipment: I hope it's as good as your other gym." Mercy showed Dina the four high balance beams, plus four low practice beams, then four sets of uneven parallel bars, and two vaulting runways, with horses, behind which was located the large foam-rubber filled pit. "We dismount into the pit when we're learning new tricks. I don't like it. But it saves the ankles. Both of which I've sprained already."

Dina nodded, then walked onto the regulation-size spring floor and bounced lightly. "Nice floor," she murmured. Then she looked over to the right wall at the edge of the floor, noticing two doors. "Is that the bathroom?" Dina asked. She liked to locate it right away in case her nerves got to her bladder.

"Yeah," Mercy said. "And the door to the left goes into the record room, where the scorekeepers work during meets. *And* where we have weigh-in."

"So how do you like Flip City?" Von asked.

Dina took a deep breath. "I think it looks perfect."

Mercy gave in to a moment of envy. "Just like you do, Dina," she thought. In a vain attempt to cover her cannonball thighs, Mercy tugged down her oversized T-shirt and shorts. Then her jealous reverie was cut short.

Joe and Eileen, the Class III coaches, walked onto the spring floor. Joe shouted, "Spread out for warm-ups!"

The eagerness to get back into the sport she loved collided with Mercy's fear of looking bad in front of her coaches. But she had no time to sort her emotions—the moment of truth was at hand. She was back at Flip City, with Von and Jules and now Dina, the place where she'd spent so much time that it was her second home. She allowed herself a brief moment of fantasy, imagining getting into her best shape ever, and scoring so well in the compulsory meets that she'd lead her Class III team to the state championships, allowing them to go on in the spring to the optional meets, where they'd cover Flip City with glory. And in the audience her whole family would be cheering for *her*, Mercy. Some dreams, Mercy thought. Some dreams. And with that, she hit the floor.

2

First Workout

September 5

As the gymnasts took seats on the spring floor, Mercy realized that there were other new faces besides Dina's. Several gymnasts from last year's Class III had left Flip City for reasons that Mercy could guess: they'd gotten too old or too involved in high school studies and activities or simply run out of time or money. Three of her former teammates had improved their skill levels last year, competed the optional season, made the obligatory overall score, and had been moved up by the coaches to compete in Class II. In their places sat new girls who had been promoted from the beginning Class IV team or had transferred from other gym schools. But a nucleus from last year's Threes still remained: Mercy, with Jules and Von in the age twelve-to-fourteen group, and Loretta, Amy, and three others in the nine-to-eleven group. They'd have to rejuvenate the old team spirit, until the new kids like Dina felt like a part of things.

Impressive Joe, curly-haired and muscular, shouted, "Warmups first! Then I'll announce the names of the new Threes and give my famous, much-loved pep talk.

For you new girls, I'm Joe McCall and this is Eileen Duffy." A petite woman with pink freckled skin and auburn bangs, Eileen looked deceptively sweet as she said, "Thanks, Joe. O.K. girls, now spread those legs and S-T-R-E-T-C-H!"

As Mercy pushed herself into starting position, she thought for a moment about Joe and Eileen, people with whom she had spent countless hours over the years. When she had started at Flip City, she had thought of them as being *old*, like her schoolteachers. Now, four years later, she felt differently about them, more the way she did about her older brother Fred and his friends. She knew Jules had a secret crush on Joe although he was married. Mercy never felt attracted to Joe, but she did find that she worked the best for him, although she couldn't satisfy him on bars. The funny thing was, Mercy matured each year but Joe and Eileen never seemed to age. Like Flip City, they stayed constant in her life.

As the girls moved into various exercise positions, Mercy saw Eileen calculating how much conditioning each gymnast needed to be back in top shape. Straining and puffing, Mercy felt the sweat spread down her back. Her T-shirt started to stick, outlining the hidden layer beneath. Quickly she glanced around and saw that Von wasn't in her most terrific shape either. And Jules, who always remained thin and flat-chested, now had grown ungainly long legs and arms, which would surely throw off her balance. Loretta also looked as though she'd had a lazy summer. But not a single Three appeared to have a genuine weight problem, except Mercy. A pink blush spread over her features to the roots of her blonde braids. Back bends, splits, straddles, protesting tendons, angry muscles, all reminded Mercy that her summer of horseback riding at Grandpa's farm hadn't been enough to keep her in gymnastic condition.

Eileen's piercing gaze moved on down the line, then rested on Dina, where her expression warmed. Mercy also took in Dina's flexibility and concentration, noticing instantly what Eileen must be seeing: Dina showed great potential.

Von watched Dina from the corner of her eye. As she measured herself against this new talent she realized she was having trouble matching the extension of Dina's splits. She turned to Mercy, and the two friends exchanged pained expressions.

After warmups were completed, the girls sat on the mats in front of the coaches, feeling hot and achy but well-stretched. Joe read the new girls' names from his clipboard. When he got to Dina, he announced that she'd moved from Albany and had competed in Class III last year. "I know you are going to bring good experience to our team, Dina. Some of our girls have never been to a Class III meet, and we have our first one coming in only a few weeks. We'll start with local meets, as you know. But I'll be expecting you experienced girls to be making the kind of scores that will put you into Sectionals and then into the State Compulsory meet in January. Flip City always sends some Threes to States; and this year, I think we have the kind of depth and spirit to send us *all*. Marion, Eileen and I believe that this team has the stuff to bring home the state trophy for Flip City."

"Right!" The Threes shouted as they always did to Joe's psych-up speeches. Mercy grinned at Dina, then let the grin die on her face. Tense and sober, Dina looked as though Joe had just dropped the whole burden of Flip City's future on her back.

"So, Dina," Joe continued, "we're glad to have you. How does Flip City compare to your gym back in Albany?"

Dina pursed her lips, searching her mind for a calm intelligent answer. "Uh, this one is really nice. Not as big. But good floor. I like the big windows . . . for the sun. . . ." She swallowed hard.

"Good." Joe smiled, taking pity on her shyness. "All gyms have the same equipment, I guess. But at Flip City we like to keep something else in stock. I mean team pride and unity. Eileen and I will work you hard, and we'll expect results. We'll help each of you to reach your personal best. But we think gymnastics is a team sport. We support each other at workouts and at meets. That's how Marion Rothman runs Flip City. Right?"

"Right!" the old-timers echoed, smiling at the awe-struck new nine-year olds and transfers.

"One more area I want to cover up front," Eileen added. "Marion, Joe, and I think behavior and sportsmanship are as important as how high you score. If anyone balks at a routine or throws a temper tantrum or tries some weeping and wailing over a score, that girl is out of the gym, out of the meet, even if your parents are watching. Those are Marion's rules. O.K.?"

As Dina nodded slowly, she rubbed her clammy

hands up and down on her calves to generate some friction. More than once in the past years, she'd been performing on the beam, and had frozen with fear and nerves. Now she was training in a gym where the kids figured she was either stupid or tongue-tied, and the coaches would bounce her out if she couldn't finish her routine.

Joe stood up. "O.K., first local meet comes in three weeks. We'll spend the workout reviewing the compulsory routines. You girls in the back row, go do the floor exercise with Eileen. You down front, over to the bars with me."

Mercy sighed, disbelief clouding her face. After a summer of slacking off, she drew the bars first. Her personal torture rack. At her slimmest she was only passable on the appartus that required an almost boyish build with trim hips and powerful upper-body strength. Today, she knew she would wipe right out.

"Start warming up with some moves," Joe said as the group stood around the crash mat beneath the bars. "Show me some glide-kips, some hip circles, some swings. Chalk up good, start rotating."

While her teammates started, Mercy lingered at the chalk dish, working the white powder into her palms. Finally she performed a few swings on the low bar. Joe asked her, "Ready to show me the routine?"

"Me?" She glared at Joe. "Can't Jules go first?"

"It's the same exact routine as last year," Joe told her. "Won't get any easier. Jules, help me set the bars for Mercy."

Mercy knew Joe was making his point, since he and Eileen had warned her to watch her weight and stay in good shape over the break. Inhaling deeply, she positioned herself on the mat and tried the mount. But she didn't have the push to get her heavy legs over the bar, and hooked one awkwardly. "Climb over," Joe said, "and take the routine from there."

Mercy hoisted herself for the kip between bars, a swinging pull-up move that slack stomach muscles and added backside weight might make impossible. As she reached the high bar, swung, and tried to keep her legs up, stiff and pointed, she gasped to Joe, "Give me a spot!" Joe helped her defy gravity with a hard push on the behind.

With the high bar pressed into her belly, Mercy swung into a front hip circle, a cast sole circle, and a half-turn. She sucked air as friction burned her palms. When she swung through between the bars on the counter-swing, her thighs smacked the lower bar smartly. She pulled up onto the bar for the stoop circle, into a straddle glide-kip, a killer move with legs spread in a V. Her shoulders strained cruelly, and she sweated through the chalk on her palms. She swung desperately, but slipped. Her rear end hit the mat with a loud splat. Mercy slumped over.

"Next time ride the bar longer," Joe said. "Now dismount."

Mercy found the strength to rise, grasp the lower bar, underswing, and, landing on wobbly legs, give her salute.

"Well . . . a little out of condition," Joe commented.

Mercy crawled off the mat, sorry that Dina and the other new kids had seen her pathetic performance. But Dina glued her eyes to the apparatus and watched

Jules get ready. Jules tugged down her leotard over her torso and gave Mercy a sympathetic shrug. Then she performed the bar routine with lots of breaks, but no misses or falls.

"That's more like it," Joe said. "We've got three weeks to work on form and smoothness, Jules. But you'll get it."

Jules dropped beside Mercy, who was massaging her palms. Stinging blisters threatened to erupt. "You'll make it too," she whispered. "You know we always suck in September."

"Three weeks? To lose ten pounds and get those bars moves? Fat chance." She scowled. "Poor choice of words."

Joe asked Dina, "How about you give the routine a try?"

Silently Dina chalked up while Joe cranked the bars closer for Dina's petite frame. Then she planted her feet precisely on the mat. A small smile bloomed on her lips. Mercy and the other girls watched, mesmerized, as Dina flew through the swings and circles and kips so rapidly and fluidly that she'd dismounted into a perfect salute before her team could accept what they were seeing. Joe stood in a trance.

"That was *so* good," Loretta murmured.

"Yeah, incredible," Jules agreed. "What form!"

Mercy felt a hot surge of envy rise in her throat, but she gulped it down.

"Uh, Dina," Joe said, "that must be your best event, right?"

Dina nodded, knowing she had to make a short speech or the kids would think she was a complete snob. "It is. I'm O.K. on floor and not as strong on vault. But . . . I clutch on beam. Really bad. My scores got so low at meets . . . that I couldn't go on in Optionals." She exhaled, unable to continue.

Instantly Mercy felt a warm spot kindle in her heart for Dina. "Hey, we've all got our weak events," Mercy said. "Beam's a killer for a lot of us. Can we see that bars number again, in slo-mo instant replay?"

The girls giggled. Dina grinned. She shook out her arms and shoulders with relief, then mounted the bars for a repeat. Mercy watched with renewed admiration. Then she realized that Dina had actually made a talk of three or four consecutive sentences. She wondered why Dina was so shy, why her talent didn't give her all the confidence she needed. Maybe Dina *did* have a real weakness on beam—but Mercy sensed there was more to it than that.

After an hour, the group rotated to the vault area. Jules told Dina, "You can do the bars almost perfectly. It's my second favorite event, after floor."

"And my worst," Mercy added. "Any ideas about how to help me stay off the mat?"

Dina raised her large brown eyes up to the two taller girls flanking her. They were nice, and might actually like her someday. "I'll try and show you whatever I can."

Later the three girls watched Von perform her final vault, a handspring. She shot forward on her landing and tripped, making friction burns on her elbows and knees. Swallowing the pain, she muttered a silent curse before she got up and regained composure.

"Hey Von," Mercy said as they walked along the

runway. "Don't feel *too* bad. I wiped out on my butt doing a kip."

"Yeah?" Von shook her head. "I have to work on my arm strength—I'm in a real slump."

"It's always like this at first workout," Mercy replied. "We'll get it all back."

Von gave Mercy a wry grin. "Maybe I'm getting too old for this?" Von was, in fact, at fourteen the oldest in Class III.

"Oh sure," Mercy rolled her eyes. "Washed up before she grows up. Come on, you know we'll go Optional this year. And besides, you're not too old yet."

"I know," Von said. "But I made a goal for myself. I told my parents that I would make it through Class III this year, or else I drop out of gymnastics."

Mercy was surprised. "Come on, Von, you love it here."

"I know, but I have to think about my future. If I do really well here, I can use gymnastics to get a college scholarship. But if I fail here, I'd better just go to Loyola and study."

"You can do it, Von." Mercy gave her a fake punch in the shoulder. "You can't quit Flip City."

Any more than I can, Mercy thought. She considered all the cash she'd have if she had time for babysitting and her parents didn't have to spend their money each month on tuition—cash for clothes, tapes, movies, ski trips. Then she added up all the spare time she'd have without the fifteen to twenty hours a week she devoted to training. "So why can't I quit?" she thought. "I'll never move up to the top or even be good enough to get a college deal. Why do I love this place so much?"

She thought about the soaring sensation she felt when she hit the springboard full on, flew into a perfect handspring vault, pushed fast and high off the horse and landed with her feet stuck in position, knees flexed just right, then rose into a salute. Nothing could compare to that kind of rush.

"Hey, Mercy!" Joe shouted. "Quit dreaming and take your vault! Von, cookie, get over on the beam!"

Mercy jumped. Waving goodbye to Von, she shook her limbs and positioned herself at the start of the runway. Focusing on the horse, she led off and tried to pace her strides. How soon to spring, how high to fly, arms controlled for momentum, head tucked, fast rebound off the horse, long post-flight, all compressed together in a moment in her mind. Her rusty reflexes crackled into action. From the corner of her eye, she caught a glimpse of Joe standing beside the horse, ready to throw out his arm for a spot. But Mercy's forward flip was strong and straight, her landing awkward but on target.

Joe stepped forward and put his hand on her shoulder, giving the usual criticism: "Watch your stride, and body position when you push off the horse. Keep that head down!" Then he added in a softer tone, "I expect you on *top* in vault this year. Right?"

Mercy nodded, grinning at the floor. Joe seldom gave that kind of positive assessment.

As the three-hour workout neared an end, the clock hands over the office door dragged. Mercy, Jules, and Dina, along with two younger girls, practiced their

floor routine. Mercy's lower back hurt from falls off
the bars; her ankles throbbed and her stomach
growled. Jules sat beside Mercy, rubbing her eyes
where chalk dust had gotten under her lenses. They
watched Dina performing a series of walkovers and
back extension rolls, knowing the girl had stretched
her body to the limits to give the coaches a good first
impression.

"Jules," Mercy sighed. "Are you dreaming of a hot
supper and an even hotter shower?"

Jules nodded. Then she gazed up at the penthouse.

"Marion's checking this out."

Mercy glanced at the windows. A short silver-haired
lady with a sober face and folded arms had appeared.
"She's watching Dina. I figured she would."

After her criticisms from Eileen, Dina dropped beside Mercy and Jules on the mat. Mercy told her,
"Myth Marion's checking your action."

"Huh?" Dina looked up at the window. "That's Marion Rothman?"

"Sure is. When I first started here, I had a coach
that called her Myth Marion. Guess she's the closest
thing to a myth we'll ever meet. And her eyes are
upon you." Mercy winked at Jules.

"She always makes me nervous," Jules admitted.
"Last January when we went to States, she just ap-
peared behind Eileen without warning, remember?
Really shook me up."

"I remember," Mercy said. "We'd barely qualified.
Eileen had a fit because we all fell off the beam. Maybe
she thought we made her look bad in front of Marion."

"Marion likes Joe best anyway," Jules whispered.

"My father heard a rumor that she's going to make him a full partner in Flip City, to keep him from going to another gym."

"I hope so!" Then Mercy leaned over to Dina. "Jules likes Joe a *lot.*"

Before Dina could manage a response, Eileen's steely voice rang out. "All right, all you girls line up outside the office for weigh-in. While you're waiting for your turn, give me fifty and fifty."

Mercy led the chorus of groans. Fifty pushups, fifty situps, and then a weigh-in. What a finale. Mercy wondered what break Eileen would give her on her weight limit, since she was taller. Eileen, herself slim and strong, insisted that hitting your goal weight could spell success for any athlete in running, skating, diving—almost all sports. But in gymnastics, extra pounds also increased the risk of injury. That's why Marion set weight limits. Mercy realized it was for the gymnasts' safety. Still, she detested the weigh-in.

As each girl came out of the office, she gave Mercy a rundown on her condition. Von said, "Got to drop a few pounds and work on the abdomen and upper arm strength. I'd better go back to doing Tai Chi with my brothers. Great for the abdominals."

Later Jules reported, "Same old story. Too tall, too thin. I need about eight pounds of muscle in perfect places."

When Dina exited, she said nothing. Eileen had found her in near-perfect shape. She glanced up to the viewers' gallery and saw her father watching her. She pretended she didn't see him, so he wouldn't expect her to wave or act dumb. She watched a new group of girls doing warmups on the floor, supervised by the Boss Lady. Marion was putting the Twos and Ones through their paces, and staring pointedly at any girl who was not stretching to her fullest degree.

Dina studied the advanced girls who'd already earned the right to Marion's expert attention. Then she stole another look up at her father. "Right, Pop," she thought. "She's not my coach. Not yet. But just give me a year."

As Mercy stood next to the office door, she fought nausea and told herself, "You're getting crazy over this scale." But when she reviewed her positive assets— clear skin, excellent health, and above-average grades—she felt she'd give them all up to see that scale needle drop to a divinely low mark. That *is* crazy, she thought. But why *can't* I have it all?

Eileen called Mercy in and measured her. "Five feet, four and a half. Up almost two inches. And you're thirteen." Eileen bent over her chart entries and made a calculation. "We can raise your goal weight about up to this. . . ." She wrote the magic number at the bottom of Mercy's chart and held it up in silence. Mercy gulped and nodded.

"O.K., let's see where we stand. Strip to your leo and give me the picture." Mercy peeled off her damp T-shirt and shorts, then stepped on the scale. She lowered her eyes, trying to control the hot flush creeping across her face. "Tell me how much," she said. "I can't look."

Eileen's voice was compassionate but firm. "You have to be down ten to compete, Mercy. And if you want to go Optional this winter and score well, you'll have to take off another five. And build your upper body strength."

Down ten just to compete? Mercy fought back despair.

"Weight control is discipline," Eileen continued. "And you know you can't succeed as an athlete without discipline. I think you're a great team member. But Marion's the boss when it comes to weight limits. And she's right."

Mercy nodded. "I can do it," she said.

"Sure you can. Go to your doctor and work out a good sensible diet. It's over three weeks before the first local meet. That's not a lot of time, but I think you can just make it. And do a series of lifts with your hand weights at night. Add twenty-five to what you did last year."

Mercy grabbed her clothes and headed for the door. Eileen stopped her. "You know Marion is tough. If you don't maintain your weight and condition, she won't string you along."

Mercy clung to the doorknob. "You mean you'd drop me?"

"Joe and I don't make the rules. Just think positive."

"Right," Mercy responded glumly.

As she headed for the changing room, Mercy passed the Boss Lady, who paced the floor, completing her advanced warmups. "Hello, Mercy," she said. Mercy said hi and smiled. Marion scanned her body with her intense hazel eyes. Mercy knew that Marion saw everything—and didn't think she had the discipline to

get back into competition shape. Big shot Boss Lady
. . . then Mercy realized that due to her summer
growth, she now looked down on Marion Rothman.

Von saw her mother waiting in the family's Toyota
wagon. After ten years in the West, Loan Nguyen still
spoke with a strong Vietnamese accent. "Hello, girls,"
she said to Von and Jules. "How did you do today?"

"Hi Mrs. Nguyen," Jules said. "Guess we've got a
long way to go before the first meet."

Von agreed. "Got to go back to Tai Chi, and cut out
the goodies."

"You do it," her mother replied. "This year you go
to the state meet. Bring home that big gold statue!"

"You mean the first place trophy?" Von said. "Joe
thinks we can. I want to get a medal in beam, maybe
in all-around."

"This may be our year," Jules agreed. "And some
of the new girls look good, especially Dina. She's incredible on bars."

"Yeah? How did she do on beam?" Von asked.

"Well, she was really nervous tonight. Fell a lot.
Nowhere near as good as you are. But her all-around
could be super."

"Uhmmm." Von felt a secret satisfaction that she
was still queen of the killer beam. But she wanted to
see Dina get *almost* as good. Then they could learn
from each other, psych each other up at meets, and
improve the team all-around. "I'll have to watch her
next workout," she told Jules. "Keep on eye on the
competition."

* * *

Jules said goodbye to the Nguyens as they let her off in her driveway. She dragged herself into the kitchen, where Evalene waited with a hot plate. "Hi. Where's everybody?"

"Hello Jewel. Your father is at the bank for regular Monday meeting. Your mother went to Opera Board. Grandfather went to Church Council. Don't fuss with those meatballs. Eat while they're nice and warm!"

"How about Grandmother?"

"She's in the den watching TV. Want to go eat by her? I fix up a tray."

"I'm too tired right now," Jules admitted. "Is she O.K. today?" In the last few years Jules's grandmother had developed severe arthritis, making it difficult for her to get around.

"She's O.K. So how did we do tonight?"

"Not too bad considering I really did grow four inches."

"Yeah? My lovely tall girl!"

"Eileen says I should put on eight pounds of muscle."

"We work out in the billiard room, with the weights."

"I know. But I have so much homework this year. Mrs. Elliot says that if I want to pass the secondary school exam and get into Rosemary Hall for ninth grade, I really have to work." Jules blew gently on a speared meatball. "I could just stay at Winchester, you know. I like it there. Who needs boarding school? I could live at home with you and compete at Flip City."

Evalene sat beside Jules. "Finish this broccoli," she

directed. "I know you got nice friends here. And Winchester is a good little school. But this Rosemary Hall, your mother says it's the best place for you. You go, meet other wonderful young ladies from all around, learn to be strong, stand alone. Your mother says the best time of life was when she went to that school."

"I'm not Mother. I'm a social zero."

"Don't talk down on yourself. You learn at Rosemary Hall not to depend on other people forever."

"Oh, you'll always be here," Jules smiled.

"Maybe. Maybe not. But you can't count on it, Jewel. You pass that exam."

Jules forced herself to finish her dinner. "So this is my last year at Flip City? Then I'll be too tall. Tall at Rosemary Hall." Her throat felt swollen. "I wish this year would never end." She swallowed her last bite. "But if it has to end, I'll show Mother that I can end it on top with a medal. I'm going to States. And Flip City's going to take the Class III trophy."

During the ride home in the Dibellas' Ford, Mercy and Dina sat together in the back seat. Mercy did the same grumbling she'd do if her own family were listening. "I'm starving. And my back kills. Aren't you about dead?"

"Uh-huh." Dina's voice was weak with fatigue.

Mr. Dibella interjected from the front seat, "Dina, I saw that Marion Rothman only coaches the Class IIs and Is. Sure hope we won't waste this year."

"No!" Dina replied. "Joe and Eileen are great."

"You could be Class II now," her father continued. "If you'd really put all your effort into beam."

"Maybe." Dina fell silent. She didn't like to be reminded of how badly she'd done tonight, how many slips, tremors, and falls she'd taken, until Eileen told her to give it a rest. The old fear of the beam was back, worse than ever.

"So what did this Eileen say about your weight and physical condition?" Mr. Dibella persisted.

Wearily Dina answered: "Weight's O.K. More upper body power. And my balance. That stuff." Her voice faded into darkness.

"Right. Weights. And a practice beam. Mom and I are having the basement room refinished as soon as we can. Then we'll have you down there working on all those problems."

As they drove beneath the light on Mercy's street, she could glimpse Dina's small sober face. A wave of pity washed through her. But why? Didn't Dina have the talent and body she'd die for? "Thanks for the ride," she whispered. But Dina had nearly dozed off.

When Mercy walked into her living room, she found her parents in their usual easy chairs, watching the news.

"Hi honey," her mother said. "Want me to come sit at the table with you?"

"That's O.K. I have lit. and history to read."

Mercy grabbed her bookbag. In the kitchen she found leftover casserole in the oven, green beans on the back burner, salad and carrots in the fridge. She filled a plate with extra tuna, minimum noodles, maximum vegetables. As she poured a tumbler of skim milk, her brother Ernie arrived in search of snacks.

"Mercy, you going to eat the rest of this casserole?"

"This is all I'm allowed. Take it away."

"Great. Coach says I have to put on some pounds."
Ernie ate large forkfuls of noodles.

"Maybe I should have gone out for football?"

"You'd probably get more playing time than me."

"Very funny. I had a rotten weigh-in. And my routines look like garbage. Be sympathetic."

"You always sound like this in September. How's
the new girl? That Dina?"

"On three events, she's the best in our class. In fact,
she could be doing Class II bars and floor. She could
take our team all the way this time at States. If she
doesn't fall apart on the beam. Of course, I won't even
be *on* the team—if I don't qualify at weigh-in."

"Oh. Yeah." Ernie knew he and Mercy fought the
same battle in different directions. He grabbed a can
of soda and left her in peace.

Mercy propped open her history text. In the silence
of the kitchen alcove, she chewed slowly and forced
herself to read.

3

Shaping Up
September 30

At the close of the Friday workout, Mercy faced her pre-meet weigh-in. She and Eileen watched the scale needle slide down and stick. After three and a half weeks of dieting, Mercy had plateaued at a loss of eight. Eileen entered it on her chart.

"Sorry, Mercy. You have to miss tomorrow's meet. You know the Threes have another local meet at Jacobsen's in two weeks. I'm sure you can hit your mark by then."

Mercy bit her lip, then turned to hide her face. "I tried." The excuse caught in her throat.

"Of course you did. Next week Joe and I are going to start you all on some optional tricks. We think you'll all qualify this fall, Mercy. You'll just have to really work for it."

Mercy nodded, but wondered how she'd ever learn an optional bars routine, one with more difficult tricks, when she could hardly make it through the compulsory one?

Avoiding the eyes of her teammates, Mercy crept over to the corner of the gym and slumped on a mat.

She had to wait for Dina to get checked, and Mr. Dibella was late anyway, so she watched the Ones warm up on bars.

They were *good.*

Mercy was especially fond of Shelley Steiner, the best of the Ones, who had made it to the Nationals last year in her age group. Everyone at Flip City knew that Shelley was almost too good for the gym. She should be working with a gym that fielded an Elite team, the highest difficulty level, required for a gymnast to qualify for the national team. But the Steiners couldn't afford to send her away; and Shelley was devoted to Marion Rothman. Mercy realized that Shelley, a sophomore, could always use gymnastics as a springboard into a college scholarship. She gazed at Shelley's sculpted muscles and jazzy red curls and knew she'd never be that skilled. But no one could be jealous of Shelley, who'd worked since she was six, coming back from minor injuries over the years, demanding that Marion push her as far as possible. Shelley had the stuff of a champion.

With Marion speaking the commands and corrections, all the Ones watched Shelley perform a difficult backwards mount, handstand pirouettes, a straddle back, release moves considered tough even for men. Oh, Shelley was flying. Mercy could see the adrenaline pumping in the color that flushed her freckled cheeks. And this was only a workout. At meets, Shelley was even more incredible.

Suddenly Shelley over-rotated her dismount and missed her footing. The speed and force of her botched landing sent her crashing off the mat against a cable. Marion lurched out, trying to grab her, but failed. Mercy could *hear* Shelley's ankle snap.

As Shelley's scream shot through the gym, Joe dashed over from the vault, and several parents ran onto the floor. But Mercy only had to look at Marion to see that they couldn't help her. Marion seemed to be in almost as much pain as the girl lying at her feet.

As the fathers and girls hovered around Shelley, Mercy asked Marion, "Should I run upstairs for a cold pack?"

Marion snapped back, "Yes! Run!" She never looked up. As Mercy ran toward the office, she heard Shelley cry out, "But it *can't* be broken. I've done that dismount a thousand times!"

When Mercy came down with the cold pack, she bumped into Dina, who had been inside the weigh-in room when Shelley fell. "What is it?" she asked Mercy. "I can't see over the crowd."

"It's Shelley Steiner," Mercy said. "You don't want to see it, Dina. Wait here for me."

So Dina lingered near the exit, awaiting her father, knowing that Mercy was right about her—she didn't want to see.

Later, in the back seat of the Dibellas' car, Mercy tried to get the sight of Shelley's grotesque ankle out of her mind.

"It was a freak accident," she told Dina. "I'll bet Shelley's out for half the season. I never saw a break like that in the gym before. But it can happen to anybody, I guess."

"We won't let it bother us tomorrow. At the meet. We just have to do our best," Dina said resolutely.

"The meet? I forgot all about it, I got so shook."

"Sure. We can drive."

"I'm out. Bumped. Didn't hit my goal." Mercy spoke the words bitterly but calmly. Her bad news didn't seem so monumental considering what had befallen Shelley.

"Oh." Dina spent the rest of the ride in miserable silence.

Back in her own kitchen, Mercy found Mom's note. "We drove down to catch the boys' football game. Be home around ten. Food in fridge." Famished, in spite of the night's events, Mercy piled a plate with cold chicken and salad, then dialed her best friend, Chrissie. "Can you come over?" She exhaled a sigh. "I need company desperately."

"Desperately?" Chrissie, having patiently followed Mercy's gym career, knew the miserable tone in her voice. "I'll get my sister to drive me. I'll bring my new tapes. I need work on my moves before the Pep Dance."

"Great. Come as soon as you can."

As Mercy munched, she thanked God for Chrissie, who although skinny and nonathletic, had sympathy for Mercy's complaints. This night Mercy couldn't stand to be alone.

The following morning Mercy's depression returned. As she prepared her breakfast of one egg, one piece of dry toast, and an orange, her brothers stumbled into the kitchen. Fred limped slightly and kept rotating his shoulders. Ernie coughed from his fall allergies. "We are some prize specimens," Mercy thought. Since her brothers had gone out for a post-game party, Mercy had not seen them before she fell asleep last night.

"Mom told me you lost," she said. "Did you both play a lot?"

Ernie answered, "Fred was spectacular. Except that whenever he shagged a pass, Middletown's defense tap danced on his body."

Mercy noticed Fred did look sore and bruised. Since he was a receiver, he often ran into the opposition's heavy traffic.

"Are you really O.K., Fred?"

"Sure. Get the milk, Ern?"

"But Fred," Mercy continued, "aren't our guys supposed to block for you?"

"Wow," Ernie said with a grin, "she's got the whole idea of the game! Except our blockers aren't always as good as Fred." Ernie poured two huge bowls of cereal, then passed the milk to Fred.

"Ernie, did you play? Did you get hurt?"

"Hulk Boyle, our mammoth tackle, stepped right on my foot. On the bench."

"Yeah? Didn't Coach put you in at all?"

"A few plays at the end. When the game was hopeless."

"Hey, he did great," Fred said, waving his spoon.

"Well, on to the really important part. How was the post-game activity?"

"Caren had a cold," Fred said. "So I went alone. Ernie made some of his best plays, though. With Marylee."

"Not a touchdown," Ernie replied, blushing. "Probably a field goal."

"So when's your first gym meet?" Fred asked while smearing peanut butter on his toast. "Isn't it today?"

"Yeah. I got bumped."

"What's this?" Ernie frowned. "An injury?"

"No. Still up two crummy pounds. All the Class IIIs are in this meet, even the little kids. Except me."

Ernie stopped eating and looked at his sister who had spent her life trying to stay trim and limber while he'd tried to put on muscle and play as well as Fred. But he couldn't think of anything to say that wouldn't sound mushy. Fred, the optimist, spoke up. "Hey, I know that sucks, but you'll work off two pounds in no time. Next meet, you'll be outstanding."

"I *did* work, Fred," Mercy cried, "and everybody at the gym thinks I'm a loser." To her surprise, tears stung her eyes. She turned and stared out the window to hide them.

Embarrassed, Ernie snapped at her, "You know football's worse. You run your buns off and get creamed at practice, so you can sit out for the game. At least in gymnastics every player gets a chance to score."

"Sure, if you can get in the meet," she whispered. She headed for the hall, tired of watching them stuff their faces.

"So where are you going?" Fred called to her. "Big plans?"

"Who cares. Guess I'll call some girls, try and get to the mall and shop."

"Thought you wanted to be a big-time athlete. Now gymnastics is too tough for you?"

"It *is* tough!" Mercy said. "Gymnasts are the best athletes of all!"

"Maybe so," Fred said, tossing the cereal carton in the air. "You want to get into the league with the big boys, but you don't really want to work hard enough to get your face on the Wheaties box."

"Yes I do!"

"Then show me how much. Get into your sweats and running shoes. We'll bike over to the Franklin track, run a few miles, then bike home and do some weights."

"I'm no long distance runner," Mercy protested. "I can't keep up with you guys."

"You'll do your best," Fred said. "We'll gear down."

Ernie said, "We don't have to work out after a Friday night game. But Fred does anyway."

"Yep. How about you, Ern? Coming?"

"Don't know. Kind of humiliating to be seen running around with your kid sister."

"Oh, bull, you're afraid I might show you up!" Mercy said.

"Yeah?" Ernie winked at Fred behind Mercy's back as he carried the breakfast dishes to the sink. "O.K., I'll take you on. But we're not going to carry you home."

"Nobody will have to carry me anywhere."

* * *

The crisp fall air bit her lungs as Mercy jogged around the high school track, eating Fred and Ernie's dust. She sensed that her brothers were pacing themselves so she could almost keep up. Even so, she was wearing out fast. Ernie coughed, then said he needed a drink. Fred's knee acted up just as Mercy's gasps started to sound nasty. They all hit the bench by the water fountain.

Mercy tried to settle her heaving lungs. "You guys . . . really do this . . . every day?"

"Regular training," Fred replied. "Right, Ern?"

Ernie nodded, trying to stifle his wheezing. Mercy decided that his breathing trouble wasn't just from the exertion of running. "Ern, you sound like you're going down for the third time. It's your allergies, huh? Are they getting worse?"

"Allergic asthma," he corrected her. "It comes and goes."

"I think you should go back to Doctor Murray," Fred said.

"Cut the advice," Ernie said. "I can manage it."

"You are nuts," Mercy told him. "Why do running sports? You could do wrestling or weight lifting or . . ."

"Why do *you* do gymnastics?" Ernie countered. "You could do some other sport, or just eat pizza every night. I play football because I want to. I worked for years to get where I am today: center position on the bench."

Fred chuckled at his brother. "The guys on the bench really do count," he said to Mercy. "They're as important as the guys on the field. You have to know that if you get shaken up or hurt, there's another guy ready to go in for you. When I make a play, crawling in the mud with some guy's cleats in my face, nobody like the fans or the news people really know what I did. But Ernie and those guys on the bench know. You need that backup."

Mercy nodded, although she wasn't sure she'd agree totally if she was Ernie on the bench.

"Are we going to talk all morning?" Ernie asked. "Or are we going to burn off a little more flab?"

"Just a few more times around, huh?" Mercy begged. "At a slow steady trot?"

Fred and Ernie jogged ahead with Mercy hustling to keep up. Her calves and arches ached. Her lungs smarted after she rounded the far turn. Still, she realized that her brothers were trying to help her. And they were keeping her out of the refrigerator. As the three of them headed for the bike rack, Mercy said, "I had an idea about this afternoon. The meet's at Flip City, so I could ride over with the Dibellas. Maybe I should be there for the team? Like I could flash scores or move the springboard or something. Help them at each event."

Ernie rolled his eyes. "Oooh, you're such a great sport."

"Sounds cool," Fred said. "Go on over. I bet that new kid Dina's going to be nervous."

"She's always nervous," Mercy said. "But she likes me."

"You'd better go," Ernie said. "Everybody expects to see a Samuels sitting center bench. The family image."

Mercy smiled as she climbed onto the bike. As they

pedaled home, she thought, "Will Marion let me follow the team? Or will I just look like an even bigger loser?" As her stomach growled angrily, she wondered, "And will I live until lunch?"

After Friday night workout, Dina finished her meal quickly so she could soak in a hot tub. She'd had an excellent weigh-in, and had gotten through her beam routine with fewer faults, but she still felt blue. Not only was she upset about Mercy's missing the next day's meet, but she'd had a rotten time at school. Slowly she let her head sink into the water, then let her face float just above the surface with her eyes closed.

One girl who had befriended her at Schindler, a quiet, plumpish blonde named Sue, had been absent. Not only had Dina had no one to dress with and talk to in P. E. class, but when she came through the lunch line and scanned the cafeteria, she couldn't find a single welcoming face. She clutched her tray, panicking. Boys kept bumping into her as she stood paralyzed. Without Sue, where would she sit? At last she spotted two of Sue's friends in the corner, girls who often joined them. Taking a deep breath, Dina walked slowly to them, until they greeted her and cleared a place. Then with stomach nearly in spasm from nerves, Dina could hardly get her sandwich down. To end the day's disasters, two eighth grade boys walked home behind her, calling out teasing sexy remarks. Dina didn't know whether to keep walking and pretend she was having a nightmare, to turn and shout back at them, to run away, or to die.

On days like this Dina missed Anthony more than ever. Two and a half years. Three years next spring. Some days it seemed like ages ago he was killed. Today it seemed like last week. He wouldn't be with her at Schindler anyway, since he'd be almost seventeen. Would he look like Mercy's brother Ernie, who had driven them to Flip City a week ago when he didn't have football practice? No, Ernie was fair like Mercy, with a rash of acne. Anthony would have been olive-skinned with brown wavy hair and maybe a little moustache. Short-legged but powerful, Anthony would have been a baseball star at Franklin High. He had been so good at baseball.

Dina forced herself to stop this kind of meditating. Mom told her it wasn't good to hold onto Anthony. He wouldn't like to see her still grieving. Pop never talked about Anthony with Dina. If she mentioned his name, Pop changed the subject. Dina sat up in the tub and rubbed the callouses on her palms and soles with pumice stone. Then she finished shampooing her hair and got out.

As Dina dried under her arms and between her legs, she faced once more the signs of her growing maturity. She didn't care for these changes. She felt she had lost control of her body. Maybe it wasn't just a rumor that the harder a girl worked out the longer it took her to get her period. She figured she would give it a try.

In her bedroom, Dina put on a T-shirt from her old Albany gym club. As she combed her hair, she smiled at the framed photo of Anthony on her dresser. Where had Pop put the one of him in his Little League uniform, holding the trophy? Now he only kept photos of Dina and her sisters Rose and Theresa on his dresser.

As she turned on her radio, she heard a tap on her door. "Dina?" Rose called. "Mom's reading a story to Theresa, so we can play a game without her butting in. How about Casino?"

As Dina opened her door, Rose gazed up at her, holding a deck of cards. Lately Dina noticed Rose had been bugging her a lot, wavering back and forth between playing kiddie games with Theresa, who was still six, and trying to act grown up. For a nine-year old though, Rose wasn't so bad.

"O.K. Rose, a few games. Then you can sit on my feet while we do another fifty and fifty."

"Great, me too!" Rose said. "I can work out for soccer."

"Are you supposed to do that many situps and pushups?"

"Sure, why not?" Rose dealt quickly before Dina changed her mind. While they played cards and listened to the radio, Rose kept asking Dina about Schindler and Flip City. Dina never admitted to being shy and tongue-tied at school—so she exaggerated here and there, making herself sound like the popular winner Rose thought she was. As far as Flip City went, Dina always had tales to tell.

"Guess what happened? A Class One girl blew her dismount off the bars and broke her ankle."

"Yeah? Was it an awful break? Did she scream a lot?"

"Uh-huh. They carried her away."

Rose looked upset. "You won't get hurt like that? You're too good, right Dina?"

"I'm careful. Don't worry."

Rose studied Dina's ribbons, medals, and trophies from competition in New York. Then her gaze rested on Dina's photo of Anthony. Her eyes grew round and sad.

"Now what's wrong?" Dina asked.

"Oh, it's like I keep forgetting Anthony. I forget how he talked and stuff. I wish I remembered."

"You were just Theresa's age, a little kid. Come on, Rose, let's do our conditioning."

"It's important for athletes, isn't it?"

"Sure. Class Ones do a hundred and a hundred, even one-armed pushups. You can't be a winner if you slack off."

Rose positioned herself upon her sister's small bruised feet and Dina did situps, remembering that all of Shelley's conditioning didn't save her from falling, and all of Mercy's work didn't keep her from getting bumped. Mercy, who gave Dina the most comfort and support, was out. She'd miss her as much as she missed Sue at school.

"Rose," she asked, "are you going to my meet tomorrow?"

"I can if you want me to. My soccer match is Sunday."

"If you come with Pop and cheer for me, I'll go and cheer at your soccer match Sunday."

Rose's eyes gleamed. "All right!"

Dina finished her pushups, then looked around her

room at her poster gallery, her wall of idols, like Nadia Comaneci, Tracee Talavera, Mary Lou Retton, Phoebe Mills, and the latest stars. She'd pulled their photographs out of her gymnastic magazines. By age twelve, they were already national competitors, in the Elite Class. But Dina had barely a ghost of a chance to get to the Nationals on any level. Nevertheless, that glimmer of hope always shone in her dreams.

Rose watched Dina's gaze. "Maybe you'll be on a poster someday. Only I won't have to buy one. I can look at you anytime for free."

Dina laughed. Rose was pretty funny. Except she was wrong. "If I ever get to be a top competitor," she said. "I'd have to leave Flip City and live near a gym that had an Elite team. You have to be Elite level to be on the national team."

"You're going to move away from home?" Rose was stunned.

"No, no. I'll never get that good. Probably."

After her long erratic day and with a meet tomorrow Dina pushed away thoughts of such an uncertain future. "Rose, I have to get about ten hours sleep. See you in the morning."

Much later Dina lay awake in the dark, listening to her parents to go bed, unable to turn off the overlapping, conflicting messages which crackled in the back of her mind.

While Jules and Von rode home with Mrs. Nguyen Friday night, Jules came up with an idea. "You want to sleep over at my house tonight?" she asked Von. "Either Evalene or Daddy can drive us to pick up your uniform and stuff for the meet, then take us over to Flip City."

"Sure, that would be fun. Is it O.K. with your mother?"

"Mother and Daddy are having a dinner party tonight. I just remembered. She never cares if I have a friend over. There'll be tons to eat. We just have to say hello and then we can take all we want to eat up to my room. If you don't come, Mother will make me change and come down and be sociable. And I'm too wiped out for that tonight."

"Sure. Mother, can I stay at Jules's house?"

"We have extra toothbrushes and nightgowns," Jules added for Mrs. Nguyen. "My parents love it when I have girls over."

Loan Nguyen nodded as she stopped for a red light and considered Jules's offer. Von, her mother had decided, should see how people like the Wolcotts lived. "Von can go. Thank you Jules."

"We'll get plenty of sleep," Jules assured Mrs. Nguyen. "My room is in the back wing so you can't hear much."

Von smiled, thinking that she couldn't remember when it wasn't noisy in the small apartment above the Oriental Grocery Store where she and her two older brothers and two older sisters grew up. Sounds of deliveries and customers below meant Father was doing good business. At night the bustle of seven Nguyens in five small rooms meant all were working hard. Stillness was foreign to Von.

When the girls entered the Wolcott kitchen, they encountered a young man and woman from a catering

company preparing food for the party in progress. "Hi,
I'm Jules. Where's Evalene?"

At that moment, the kitchen door swung open. Evalene charged through, wearing a black dress with a
starched apron, with her hair slicked back into a bun.
She was holding an empty silver tray. "This is Miss
Julia," she told the caterers. "And Miss Von. Give
them dinner."

Von stared for a moment before she recognized the
officious maid as Evalene. Jules grinned to see Von's
shock. Evalene watched as the young man filled her
silver tray with hot cheese and shrimp puffs. She gave
several samples to the girls. "You eat all you want from
counters and oven, but don't touch trays. And Jules,
later go in and greet guests."

Evalene marched back through the door, balancing
a tray laden with hot canapes. As she munched, Von
said, "She called you Miss Julia."

"When she serves a party, she gets very formal."

"I never saw her without her Red Sox cap and Patriots jacket. She looks so different."

"We'd better shower," Jules said. "I'll give you clean
sweats." She led Von up the rear staircase to her room.

"Do those cooks make a lot of money?" Von asked.

"The caterers? Sure. Evalene will only work with
the best."

"I could learn to do that. I can already make things
in the café, like little spring rolls with shredded crab
and vegetables. They taste even better than those
things we just ate."

"You think you want to be a caterer?"

"Just during high school. I could do parties like this

and save a lot of money for college," Von explained. Then she realized that Jules had probably never thought about saving money for college. "But later, I think I'll study business and run a company. Maybe a bank, like your father."

Jules's eyes grew wide. She had no idea Von was so ambitious about her career. As she pulled a set of clean panties, sweatpants, and shirt from her bureau, she said, "Go on and use my bathroom first." After Von took the clothes and headed for the shower, Jules sat at her dressing table and took out her contact lenses and her detested retainer. Jules knew that Von was pretty smart, having seen her calculate scores and averages at meets in her head. But run a business or a bank? That was beyond Jules, who was having enough trouble getting through eighth grade Math Enrichment, a course for slower learners at Winchester. She pulled her long auburn hair out of a ponytail and brushed it, studying her face in the mirror. Her nose was still stubby, not elegant, and blemishes dotted her forehead. Von never seemed to worry about her face, hair, or figure. How she wished some of Von's confidence would rub off on her!

After their showers, Jules took Von down for the obligatory party visit. They found Kate Wolcott in a long black cashmere cowled dress, cigarette and drink in hand. "Here come our young lady athletes!" Kate spoke loudly. The guests turned to stare.

"Hi Mother, Von's sleeping over tonight. All right?"

Von was almost as surprised to see Mrs. Wolcott looking so glamorous (since she usually encountered her in slacks) as she had been to see Evalene in uniform. "Thanks for having me, Mrs. Wolcott," she said.

Kate beamed at Von so all her perfect teeth showed. "We love Julia to have company. Please take all you want to eat from the kitchen. I know you have to keep up your strength. Julia, you look terribly tired." Kate told the women standing beside her, "They do the most strenuous things in their gym."

"We'll be fine, Mother. 'Night." As Jules led Von to the kitchen, she felt a bit annoyed. No one but Evalene had seen her do anything strenuous in a gym for years. Evalene drove to practices and came to meets. At least Daddy liked her being in sports and sometimes dropped in on a meet to catch a routine. But Mother didn't care for Flip City at all. Sometimes she could be so phony.

Later, closeted in Jules's room with platters of food and a six-pack of diet soda, the girls satisfied their huge appetites. They took turns passing around the Myoflex and Vitamin-E cream, working on their strained muscles and callouses.

"Can you believe our first meet's tomorrow?" Jules asked. "I fell off beam about five times during one routine. I've still got two blisters. I know I'll rip them on bars."

"What I can't believe," Von replied, "is that we sit around and talk like this! My other friends think I'm crazy to give up private high school for the gym."

"I'm glad you have." Jules smiled. "And you'll make it at Bush. You're probably the smartest one in your class."

"No way. But I got lucky. All my teachers are good in the honor track. If I can hold onto an A average at

Bush and make it into Class I optionals, I think I can find a college that will give me a deal. Don't you think so?"

"Oh sure. Joe says lots of gymnasts are getting scholarships these days. Von . . . do you want to go far away?"

Von's dark brows rose as an eager gleam flashed from her round eyes. "I'm going to the best school, no matter how far."

"Don't your brothers go to City College?"

"Yes, it's fine for them at home. They go out at night, see who they want. My father doesn't bug them. But I'm his 'little girl' and he's really strict. When I grow up, it will be better if I go away on my own."

Von stretched out on the carpet and started the abdominal exercises she did each night. Jules was too tired to join her. "But Von, what if you get homesick? Without any Vietnamese friends?"

"I can't worry about that," she replied resolutely. "I'll be too busy studying and training for the gym team, traveling to competitions. And meeting guys." She sat up and grinned.

"Oh. Guys. Sure." Jules thought about the handsome male gymnasts pictured in their magazines, guys who looked like Joe. "I guess there'll be some tall guys at Rosemary Hall, since it's got a boys school. It's got to be better than Winchester, as far as boys go."

"Not too many hunks there?" Von asked.

"Oh, some of the guys in the upper school are cute, but they only talk to older girls. Know what I have in eighth grade? Twelve girls and nine boys. Not one comes past my chin."

Von giggled. "So this boarding school should be wonderful, huh?"

"Mother went there and loved it." Jules kept her fears to herself. How would Von ever understand?

"You come home every holiday and tell me what it's like to live with handsome guys. Then I can daydream until I go away to college." Von smiled at Jules, who appeared to her to have no problems. The financial pressures which ruled Von's life never entered into Jules's thoughts. Good thing Jules was so nice; she couldn't be jealous of her.

"I'll tell you all about it," Jules replied, knowing she'd have no social success to report. "Guess we better get some sleep. For the meet."

After Jules drifted off, she had a funny dream in which she dressed Von in her clothes and sent her off to Rosemary Hall in her place. No one at home noticed, except Evalene, who had thought up the switch, until the mid-term report came home with straight As.

4

Qualifying Meet
October 1

When Mercy arrived with the Dibellas for warm-ups, they discovered the Flip City parking lot already jammed with out-of-town cars. After they squeezed the Volvo into a place by the dumpster, a small parade formed: Mr. Dibella, holding the notebook in which he recorded every move of Dina's career; Rose, carrying a large tin of brownies her mother had made to sell at the parents' goodie table; Dina, silently toting her gym bag; and Mercy. As Mercy gazed up at the azure sky and sniffed the sweet breeze, she realized she might now have been at Schindler Field waving a pompom and screaming her brains out for her team on the field. Instead she was hanging out at Flip City breathing in Eau de Sweat Sock. It was unusual for a girl to get bumped and still want to rotate with the team and assist. Joe and Marion might not let her help. Then what? Sit in a corner and wait out the meet? Why, she thought, am I doing this?

As they approached the entrance, Dina turned and smiled her half smile. "It's great . . . that you came."

Mercy knew. She was here for her team, her friends.

The changing room was crammed full of gymnasts when Mercy and Dina shoved their way through to a locker. Von, Jules, Loretta, Amy, and the rest all cheered to see Mercy.

"Did Marion change her mind?" Von asked.

"No. Just thought I'd get you all psyched."

"Yeah? That's super!" Jules said.

"I better check with Joe and see if I can go around with you."

"I saw him go upstairs," Jules said. "With Marion."

"Marion's here? For a Class III compulsory?" Mercy couldn't remember Marion's ever having been at a local meet. She shot a glance at Dina, whose face had frozen. "O.K., I'll run up and talk to her. See you!"

Mercy climbed the stairs to the crowded gallery, already filled with parents. The door to the office was closed, so Mercy knocked. Joe answered, stepping outside.

"Hi Mercy, how are you doing?" he asked with a smile.

"I came with Dina," Mercy said. "So I wondered, could I go around with the team? Help you set up for events?"

"Sounds good to me. I can use your help. Eileen had to take the Twos down to their meet in Stamford. You can be my assistant."

Mercy brightened. "What should I do?"

"Help me cue the music for the floor routines, pull the springboard after the beam mounts, adjust height on the bars."

"O.K."

"I'll place the springboard and do the spotting on

vaults, but you stay in back of the runway, keep the less experienced kids ready and focused."

"O.K. Joe, should I ask Marion? You know I got bumped."

Joe put his hand on Mercy's shoulder. "No, I said it's O.K."

The two of them dashed down to the floor, where Joe called the other four teams' names and made rotation assignments for warmups and competition: "Gymnettes from Jacobsen's Gym. Valley Girls from Valley Gymnastic Center. Marvelles from Middletown YWCA. Flyers from Hamden Gym." The coaches came up and organized their teams.

Only Flip City didn't have a catchy team name or emblems emblazoned on their uniform backs. As a kid starting out, Mercy had suggested they call the team the Marionettes. She thought that was so clever. Marion didn't buy it. Over the years, Marion had scoffed at costly leos and warmup uniforms, ordering plain navy with a gold stripe on the side. "I only care about what's inside the suit," Marion had told Mercy. Now Mercy was starting to see Marion's point.

As Flip City warmed up on bars, Mercy helped adjust the height for Jules. While Jules worked out, she sat beside Von and asked her, "Your folks make it today?"

"Real busy day at the store. And both my brothers have Saturday jobs. But I never notice who's here."

"That's true. You have incredible focus. How come I don't see Evalene down front?"

Von spoke softly so Jules wouldn't hear. "Mr. Wolcott drove us over. I slept at Jules's house last night, while the Wolcotts had this big dinner party. We all slept pretty late. After we had lunch in the kitchen with Evalene, Mr. Wolcott told Evalene to stay and clean up from the party, and he'd take us to the meet. We had this idea he was going to stay and watch Jules, but he just said, 'Good luck, see you at five.' I don't know. It's like Jules and her parents don't get much straight between them."

Mercy agreed. "But it's just as well that he didn't stay for the meet. With her father and Marion both staring at her, Jules could have a breakdown."

"Yeah, and he'd never get a seat in this mob." The girls observed the overflowing gallery, the families lining the walls around the spring floor and the beam mats. Even the exits were blocked. After Joe got on the mike and announced that spectators *must* clear all doorways, families tried to shift. But they found it nearly impossible to get reorganized. Small siblings tumbled on mats. The noise grew.

"It's a madhouse," Mercy said. She looked over at Dina, who was warming up on the spring floor near her father and sister, who perched at the edge. "Dina's going to do a dive-roll right into her father's lap."

Von studied Dina. "She's still dynamite on floor."

"Yeah, I know. She cruises on bars and vault. But she dies on the beam. She even has to force herself through a simple warmup. We've got to try and figure out what's bugging her so bad, and give her some of your cool."

"Sure," said Von. "Except how are we going to figure her out? She hardly talks."

Mercy shrugged. "Beats me. But I'm working on it."

After Jules finished her bars warmups, she pulled on her uniform jacket and sat beside Mercy and Von. "How'd I look?"

"About six times better than me," Mercy said.

"Not true," Jules grinned. "We're going to miss your points a lot, especially in the over-all scoring. I know it's just a local meet. But still . . .

"Did you check out the judges?" Jules said. "All four of my worst scores last year came from the Thin Black Guy and the Picky Blonde. And there they are!"

"But the Picky Blonde scores high on floor."

"Not for me," Jules replied. "The Pleasant Plump Lady gave me my best last season." She gestured toward the fourth judge, a muscular man in the regulation blue blazer. "It's Pop-Eye that kills you on bars. I saw him give a girl a 3."

Dina strolled over after her floor warmup and overheard their comments. "We gave our judges nicknames too," she said.

"We call those three the Thin Black Guy, Pop-Eye, and Shorty." Jules told her. "They're tough. But the Picky Blonde is the worst."

Dina rubbed her palms tensely. "Looks like my turn to warm up on beam." With that, she vanished into the crowd.

A while later Dina managed to make an inconspicuous trip to the bathroom. The palpitations had started, along with the strangling feeling in her throat.

Her warmup on beam had gotten shakier with each pass. As she leaned against the sink, she forced down even breaths to settle her heaving stomach. She then pressed cold wet toweling to her face and neck. Her hair lay damp with the sweat of fear. She avoided facing herself in the mirror. Then a rap sounded on the door.

"Hey, is Dina Dibella in there?"

Dina recognized Mercy's voice and had to let her in.

Mercy tried to hide her shock. Dina, leaning under the fluorescent tube by the sink, looked sallow, sweaty, and tense.

"Did you get sick?" Mercy asked.

"No. I'm O.K. Just a little nervous."

"Oh. Maybe I'd better get Joe."

"No!" Dina's eyes met Mercy's. "Don't say anything to him." Just then Joe's voice sounded over the mike, announcing the assembling of teams for the national anthem. "It's line up."

"Dina, are you sure you're O.K.?"

"Sure." Dina squared her shoulders and marched out the door. Mercy followed, more confused than ever by Dina's silence.

As the teams were split into age groups, the elevens and under headed first for the vault, while the twelves and up went to the bars. Mercy assisted in adjusting bars for the Flip City girls in her rotation. She recognized many girls from the Gymnettes, Flyers, and Marvelles, all of whom had competed against her team last season. She wondered how much they'd improved. The really big winners from last season were gone, having moved up to Class II. But two of the kids sitting beside Dina awaiting the bars greeted her cheerfully. They'd both had growth spurts like Jules, so that Mercy hardly recognized them.

While she watched their routines, Mercy had time to become conscious of the crush of spectators hovering even closer than usual to the apparatus. When Mercy performed, she blocked out everything but the equipment. Now she saw faces and bodies packed on all sides, rustling, coughing, mumbling. She jumped at each violent crash of the springboard during each vault, then started at each burst of applause when the vaulter saluted. How could Dina close her eyes and ears to all but the perfect timing needed to complete moves on the bars? How did any of them concentrate in this atmosphere thick with sweat, excitement and airborne bodies?

Then Dina was on deck. As Mercy adjusted her bars height, she gave her an encouraging grin: "Do it up, Dina."

Dina chalked up her hands and zeroed in on the equipment. She shot into her mount, swung with fast assured precision back and forth; she hit her belly-beat with such force that the rebound could have sent her into a handstand on the bar. She swung through to a long hang kip from the high bar and flowed instantly into a perfect dismount, which she stuck without a waver.

As Dina landed an impressive distance from the bars, the crowd watched, fascinated. A loud burst of applause filled the gym. Dina retired to the mat, lowering her eyes as her teammates patted her and cheered. The team listened as Joe gave her his critique. "Good job! A few tenths for breaks in your leg extension, legs parted on the stoop circle, minor balance problems on the dismount. We'll polish them."

Resisting her envy, Mercy stood beside Dina. How high could she score on such an exercise out of the perfect ten? Together they waited through the following Gymnette's routine, until the girl beside the judges held up the standard with Dina's score: a 9.1!

Mercy was mute with shock. Never had she seen a higher bars score at a Class III compulsory meet. Dina, she realized, was nearly perfect on bars. They were so lucky to have her. She could make all the difference in the team's all-around.

Dina smiled at her team's cheers, then glanced at Mercy. She hoped her score wouldn't stand between her and her new friend.

Mercy told her, "Guess you'll be doing the optional bars routine next week. You sure have this one licked."

Joe listened and said, "And the rest of you will be joining her, Mercy. Got that?"

"Yeah. Got it. Flip City girls go together."

Dina exhaled, her thin lips parted, and her teeth gleamed in a smile of relief. She was a Flip City girl.

The rotation went well for Flip City. Jules, who overshot her landing on her handspring vault, got penalized for taking extra steps, but still ended up with a 7.0. Von, who still needed more punch on her push-off, nailed her landing and pulled a 7.7. Mercy ached to join them, believing that when she got her skills honed, she'd be scoring 8s, soaring powerfully high, landing solidly far down the mat.

Dina excused herself after her snappy 8.1 vault and dashed to the bathroom. As time neared for her beam, she remained closeted in the toilet, clutching her knees and talking herself through her panic attack. "I am good, I am solid and limber. I won't freeze or break focus. I won't fall and break my neck." She pulled up her leo, went to the sink and sponged off. Pains throbbed in her lower abdomen. She prodded her belly, thinking she'd hit the bar too hard. Would these pains distract her when she stretched back for a walkover on the beam? Her head swam dizzily. But her time had run out. Dina hurried back to the mat just as Mercy set the springboard for Von's mount.

Dina always admired Von's poise on the beam, hoping someday she could copy her style and confidence. She watched Von's moves: the smoothness of her body wave, the height of her kicks and leaps, the swiftness of her full turn, the grace of her dance steps and poses; Von had perfect line on her scale, and held her side handstand for a solid three seconds. She exuded confidence as she poised for the back walkover. But when she reached back, she miscalculated—and slipped. As she fell, she banged her neck and shoulder hard on the beam. Dina gulped down her impulse to scream.

Stunned, Von sprawled on the mat, then rose to her knees. Joe leaned over and asked, "Can you finish?"

Von sucked in deep breaths and pushed the pain to the back of her mind. All she saw was the beam. If she made her final run and dismount, then her routine, although scored fairly low, would still count for the team's overall score. Von had always been taught to complete what she started if possible. So she crawled back up and finished her final pass and dismount. Applause for her courage greeted her salute.

The team crowded around Von while Joe felt her neck and shoulder. Suddenly Marion materialized at her side. She probed Von's bruises while she studied her eyes. "Nothing's dislocated. We can't be sure about sprains or ligaments. How do you feel, Von?"

Von lowered her lids. "I want to finish the meet."

Marion considered Von's wishes, then sent one of the ten-year-olds for a cold pack. "I'll decide if you should perform when your turn comes on floor. Sometimes an athlete has to know when to cut her losses." Von didn't speak, furious at her stupid mistake on a beam routine she could do in her sleep. Then Marion turned to Dina. "I believe you are on deck. Now go for it!"

Dina had been so absorbed in the drama of Von's injury, she had forgotten she was up next. With Von hurt, her father only feet from her, Marion right under her nose, Dina had to prove to all that she could walk the wall of her nightmares. She chanted to herself as she sucked in oxygen, "Do it up, do it up." She shook out her limbs, saluted the judges, and hit the springboard.

The plinkety-plank of the floor exercise music stopped as the rotation ended. An overflowing gym of restless spectators stared at the terrific new kid now up on beam. But Dina didn't hear their mumbled comments; she heard only the words in her head:

"I am dancing on wood wide and firm as a sidewalk."

Clinging to her concentration, she did each move in near slow motion, freezing in each pose. When the time came for her walkover, the trick that threw Von, instead of arching her spine and reaching blindly back for the beam, she halted. Then she leapt, whipping her legs in the air, and landed firm. A shudder went through her as she rose and posed.

The time-keeper beside the judge spoke the word: warning.

Dina hadn't done her final pass down the beam, but if she didn't complete her dismount in ten seconds, she'd lose valuable points. With a final push she flew down the beam, landing on the split-second with an off-balance salute.

As she walked back, she dreaded the expression on Marion's face. She turned her head to the score-flasher. No matter how badly she'd done, she had to see her score. Amazingly, she drew a 6.5.

Joe put his arm around her shoulder. "I know you were shaken up after Von fell. The judges gave you a few gifts with that score. You had about ten hesitations and breaks in form. We'll fix them eventually. Now take it easy."

At last Dina walked over to Marion. "Thought you'd freeze," Marion told her. "But you came through. That's good."

Dina's knees buckled with relief. She sat next to Mercy, whose solid presence always helped. Mercy told her, "I thought you really pulled it off."

"Thanks," Dina said. "But Jules got the same score and she did a much better routine. And Von was scoring super, until she fell."

Dina knew that if she'd fallen the way Von did, she'd never have had the courage to get up again.

After the final rotation began, Jules, Von, and Dina sat with several Flyers and Gymnettes at the edge of the floor. Mercy stood at the tape recorder, ready to cue the same tinkling tune for each exercise. Jules drew the first slot up, a bad position in the rotation since the judges liked to leave themselves room to go higher. Jules paced along the floor's edge, tugging down her leotard. Mercy told her, "Go for it, it's your best."

Jules smiled gamely. "You know they score the first routine pretty low. I'm probably in trouble."

The judges gave the nod, so Jules saluted and strode onto the spring floor. As she struck her starting pose and awaited the music's opening beat, she thought about how last year she had scored 8 on both floor and bars. Could she do it again? The tune blasted from the tape recorder. Jules mentally ran through the admonitions Eileen always chanted: "Pose the arms, chin high, extend the legs, point the toes! Feet, feet!" Eileen's voice echoed inside her head. The music carried Jules along through leaps, spins, rolls, cartwheels, and walkovers, her heart pounding with the rhythm. Then the final chord sounded just as she hit her pose. Perfect timing, perfect placement! She felt gorgeous!

Jules beamed as she heard the team cheer. If only Daddy was here to see her. . . .

In Eileen's absence, no floor coach was present for detailed criticisms. But Joe had watched Jules's routine from the vault runway. She knew he too was waiting to see her score flash. Then the standard turned: an 8.2! Mercy ran to hug her and exclaim, "Fabulous! On a first routine!" But Jules peeked across the gym and through the crowd, where she saw Joe raise his arm and give the V-sign. She ducked her head to hide her blushes. Mercy, however, saw it all.

After the competition, while scorekeepers tabulated the winners in each event, the teams huddled in groups to compare failures and estimate success. Von, who could add decimals in her head, ran down everyone's overall. Since Marion had forbidden her to compete on floor after her fall, her own tally was poor. But the rest of the Threes had done very well. A total overall score of 28 was considered the magic number which qualified the gymnast to go on to sectional and state level meets. Von asked Dina to recite her scores. She mentally added them twice. "I get 32.3! Dina, that's spectacular."

"Dina, you've qualified already," Jules said in awe.

"I bet it's the winning number of the day," Mercy added.

"Oh Dina," Loretta said. "You'll win All-around."

"Yeah," said Amy. "That means our team overall will be the best too, huh? Flip City wins!"

"Maybe not," Von said glumly. "I brought us down, and Mercy didn't compete. I don't think the team can win. But Dina can."

Mercy thought about Von's words. Dina won with a shaky beam routine. Imagine how high she could score overall with a good beam routine? If enough girls in each age group managed to qualify for States, and if each girl did her all-time best, Flip City might win Class III States. Mercy didn't think that had ever happened before. More powerful, larger gyms downstate usually won. But with Dina Dibella flying in the foreground, and the rest of the Threes bringing up a solid backfield—they had a fighting chance.

"Von," Mercy said. "I just figured it out. We can win States this year. We can. We can bring back that huge trophy."

"Wait a minute," Von said. "If you get one of the top six scores in an event, you get your *own* gold medal, on a ribbon."

"And what about All-around?" said Mercy. "Top six in each age group get their own medals for that too."

"You're right! Dina, Jules, you, and me. And Loretta, she'll be twelve."

All together the girls looked at Dina, who was studying a blister on her left palm. Dina felt their eyes upon her, but made no response. Although she knew Mercy and the others were mostly daydreaming, Dina felt the most pressure was on herself. Because winning the State All-around had become Dina's personal private goal. She was going to show them *all*.

MacArthur Wolcott waited at the exit to Flip City. When the girls piled into his Mercedes he remarked, "I arrived in time to see Miss Julia pick up a few awards, didn't I?"

"Yes!" Jules held up her prizes. "Fourth on bars, third on floor, and tied for sixth on beam. Von could have won beam, but she fell."

"I'll be all right. I have a neck brace at home."

"So how was your afternoon, Daddy?" Jules asked.

"Not too painful. I started at a new health club that all the officers at the bank have joined. I'm going to work out every weekend, and maybe one evening after the bank closes."

"Really? Daddy, you mean lifting weights?"

"Some. And swimming laps. Don't want to get old before my time, do I?"

"I think you still look pretty good," Jules smiled. But she realized that her father was turning fifty in a few months, and although he remained lean and charming, he was out of condition.

"I don't want you to mention the health club to your mother yet. You know how easily she gets upset, afraid someone will get hurt. She doesn't understand about athletics like we do."

"Well," Jules said slowly. "I think she'll wonder where you're going. I think you'd better just tell her. Besides, what if she starts grilling me?"

"You'll keep my secret," Mr. Wolcott said.

Von remained silent in the back seat, wondering why the Wolcotts came and went so much without telling each other the truth. Her parents worked together and discussed every detail of family life. But at the Wolcotts', no one seemed to know what anyone else was doing. Weird, Von thought, weird.

During the drive home, Mr. Dibella went over each event with Dina, especially her hesitations on the beam. Mercy sat in the back with Rose and listened, amazed that Dina's father could keep so many detailed performance points in his head. Then Mr. Dibella concluded, "You know, your beam work is worse. We're going to finish that playroom in the basement right away and put a practice beam down there."

"Right. I need it." Dina looked out the window.

"Dina?" Rose asked. "Can I see your ribbons?"

Dina tossed back a fistful as if they were no more important than sticks of gum. Rose examined them eagerly.

"And we know you'll be back competing in the next meet," Mr. Dibella added to Mercy. "Good stiff competition from experienced girls, that's what Dina needs most."

"Oh. right." Mercy answered. "Thanks."

"Oh, Pop," Dina murmured.

Mercy realized that Mr. Dibella's encouraging statement reduced her to a prop for furthering Dina's career. She knew however that he was right. Something was needed to ignite Dina's hunger to win.

When Mercy entered her kitchen, she found her mother finishing the gravy for the pot roast. "Perfect timing!" Mrs. Samuels said. "You can join us for a change!" The tempting smells of baking potatoes and green bean casserole filled the air. Dad, who was setting the table, asked, "How'd your team do, honey?"

"Really well. Dina won All-around." Mercy recounted the team's good points. "But Dina made two trips to the john to be sick."

"Oh no, do you think she had the flu?" Mom asked.

"She gets these panic attacks. She's so intense. Sure,

we all get uptight about competing. But with Dina, what she does in the gym seems to be the major news in her family. You guys just tell me have fun and don't get hurt."

"Maybe it's Dina that cares too much?" Mom said.

"I don't know. Her sister treats her like a star. Her father writes down her every move. Even Marion was grinning when she won the All-around, kind of like the Cheshire Cat over Miss Mousie. And now we're all counting on her to win for the team. Maybe we all put too much pressure on her?"

"You're a good girl to worry about her," Dad said. His gaze wandered to the window, where in the dusk they could just see Fred and Ernie passing the football. Mercy knew that Fred's first-string position on the team meant a lot to Dad. Mercy hardly remembered Fred without a football in his hand. Dad had probably put a little one in his crib. Mercy smiled to herself, then reflected: if the Dibellas had a strapping son like Fred then they wouldn't let it all ride on Dina. Did Fred feel really pressured to be a star? No, she decided Fred would play even if no one ever cared; he just lived for football. Then what about Von? She was number five, yet her parents expected her to succeed. And what about Mercy herself? Mercy knew that her parents were much absorbed with Fred's last season in football and his getting a college scholarship. They had little time to pay attention to her every move. Sometimes she wondered if they really noticed her at all.

"Mercy, hold up the plates. Paul, call in the boys.

Mercy, honey, quit daydreaming! Aren't you even hungry?"

As her mother served the pot roast, Mercy decided that at the moment what counted most was eating this delicious dinner. The rest of life's dilemmas could wait until later.

5

Getting through the Weekend

October 14

"**M**om, Dad? I did it! I lost ten big ones!" Mercy shouted as she burst through the front door.

"We knew you could do it!" Mom said.

"If I can just score thirty all-around at next week's meet, I'll go on to Sectional meets. Then if I hit about thirty-two, States. Eileen really grinned when she saw my weigh-in. True approval!"

"Honey, that's great," Dad said. "Are your routines better?"

"Yeah, especially the bars. Less weight really counts there. Joe was so happy when I told him, he went like this: pow!" Mercy shot up her fist and punched an imaginary cloud over her head. "So I better hurry if I'm going to make the pep dance."

"Want to eat first or shower?" Mom asked.

"I'm too excited to eat now."

"That's a first," Dad smiled.

But Mercy was already dashing upstairs, shedding sweats as she ran for the shower. As she slammed the bathroom door, she heard angry male voices from Ernie's bedroom but was too happy to care who was bawling out whom. She showered fast, blow-dried her long fair hair and fastened it back with two large barrettes. From her closet, she pulled last spring's Calvins and got the best surprise of the day: they fit. She patted her flatter tummy.

"Ernie?" she called out her door. "Can I borrow your green V-neck?" Mercy loved wearing her brothers' long saggy sweaters over tight jeans. Ernie stepped into the hall, then shrugged. "Sure, if you can come up with it."

Mercy pulled on a T-shirt to enter Ernie's room, nearly tripping over piles of books, clothes, jackets, shoes. Most of his wardrobe lay in mounds on the rug and chair. "Ern, you need a bloodhound to find anything in here."

"Not true. Don't mess up my stuff looking around."

"Very funny. Guess there's no point in checking your dresser?" She spotted the V-neck. After shaking it vigorously, she pulled it on.

"Ernie," she called, "are you taking Marylee out tonight?"

"Yeah, to a party."

"Can you drop me off first at Schindler for the pep dance?"

"Sure, but you'll have to get yourself home, since we'll be late."

"O.K. Hey, don't you have an out-of-town game tomorrow?"

"Yeah. So?"

Fred appeared, clad in aged jeans and a Franklin sweatshirt with the sleeves torn out. Mercy turned to him. "I just thought you weren't supposed to party late the night before a game."

"Yeah, if you play like Fred," Ernie said nastily. "I'll be suited up, center bench, so who the hell cares. Come on."

He pushed past Fred and dashed down the hall. Mercy grabbed her wallet and jacket. Fred smiled at her. "Did I hear you say you hit your weight goal?"

"Yep. I just have to hold on, and I'm in the next meet."

Fred said thoughtfully, "You're the real athlete. Because you do the most with what you've got."

"Oh, sure," Mercy snorted. "I'm going to be lucky to ever make it through Class III, and you're Franklin's star receiver. Dad just about lives to see you play. I'd say that puts you in the top class around here."

"Maybe," Fred admitted. "But my competition for the team spot is just some guys who happen to go to Franklin. You compete with girls from all over who kill themselves to raise their scores. I was born with the right body for football. You have to work against your body to win. So who's the best athlete?"

Mercy beamed under Fred's praise. "Somehow I don't think Mom and Dad would agree with that . . . but thanks." Then she heard Ernie yell for her, so she ran down for her ride to the dance.

At the entrance to Schindler, Mercy read, "Once you are stamped, you may not leave the gym or corridor." A table of chaperones guarded the door, recalling last year's dance when some eighth graders stashed beer in the bushes, sneaked in and out, drank, and got sick. Mercy was glad the dance was sealed; she had no use for kids who got drunk.

The dance had been in progress for forty-five minutes, but in spite of the DJ blasting the best songs, only the Student Council, sponsors, and a few kids were dancing. Mercy saw Deb, Chrissie, and three of her other friends hanging around the refreshment table.

"Hi," she called. "Why isn't everybody dancing?"

Chrissie pointed to the bleachers. "See George Feder and all those guys? They said they drank their beers in the parking lot already."

Mercy saw half the football and basketball teams looking smashed, laughing and acting macho. Mercy bought a diet cola and said, "I'm checking this out. I don't believe George would get drunk. He's been in my class since kindergarten, and he's not that big a turkey."

"Maybe you're right," Deb said. "I bet they're faking it."

The girls followed Mercy over to the bleachers. "You guys forget how to dance or what?" Mercy asked the boys.

"Too laid back," George replied in a low slurred voice. "Had a few beers. You know."

"How many?" Mercy demanded.

"Oh, uh, three."

"Sure. If you drank three beers in the parking lot, you couldn't crawl up the stairs into the school."

The boys chuckled. "Speak for yourself," Steve said. "We can hold it."

"If you can hold it," Chrissie snapped, "then why can't you dance with us?"

"Hey, we can dance." George and the boys danced around, staggering and bashing into each other and laughing uproariously.

"Terrific," Mercy groaned. "If Coach Zawicki walks in on this scene, you guys are dead meat. Come on, let's find some better company."

"Right," said Chrissie. "For this I practiced dancing?"

The girls joined other friends by the refreshment table, where they discussed whether the boys were faking it. Mercy asked, "Can they keep this up until eleven? Real drunks would have to sober up or pass out, wouldn't they?"

"Don't ask me," Chrissie said. "I don't know any real drunks."

"My big brother drinks sometimes," Deb said. "He acts loud and crazy for a while, then he falls asleep."

"How about your brothers?" Chrissie asked Mercy.

"Not Fred. He's totally dedicated to staying in training. I think Ernie's come home smashed. But he goes right to bed, so Dad doesn't see him." They watched the DJ continue to hustle. Still the action on the floor was small.

"How long can those guys keep going?" Deb asked. "For hours?"

Mercy said, "This is so dumb, waiting to see what they do."

"The music is cool," Chrissie yelled over the new record, which the DJ had turned up to ear splitting level.

"Look!" Deb shouted. "They look sick. They're running out the door."

"Hope they make it to the boys' room," Chrissie said.

Mercy rolled her eyes in dismay. "I can't wait until next year at Franklin. When we go to school with older guys, we can forget we even know these nerds."

"You mean older guys like my brother Rich and your brother Ernie?" Deb asked. "That's a big improvement?"

Some time later, George Feder returned and ambled across the gym to the refreshment table, with his face and hair soaked with water. He grinned at Mercy, then asked the girl behind the table, "Got any black coffee?"

"You know all we have is Coke. And quit dripping on the table."

"O.K., make mine straight." He told Mercy, "Good old caffeine, sobers you up."

"What did you do?" Mercy asked. "Stick your head under a faucet?"

"Yeah. After we hung out the windows. You know."

"I can't believe you guys are so gross." Mercy tried not to grin, but failed. It was hard to take George seriously.

George downed his cola in several swallows, then burped. Encouraged by Mercy's tolerance, he asked, "Want to dance?"

"Sure you won't drip on me?"

George shook his tight black curls like a sheepdog, letting droplets fly. "How's that?" Mercy had to giggle.

The DJ put on a slow song by a group Mercy loved.

Although she felt uncomfortable being one of the few couples on the floor, she wanted to let George redeem himself. As they started to dance, she put her hand on his shoulder and realized he was tall but rather bony. Her shoulders were probably better developed than his. Would he think she was too much of a jock? When he squeezed her hand trying to lead her, she worried about the dried blisters and callouses she'd gotten from working the bars.

"Are you going out for basketball again?" she asked, hoping to distract him from her ugly hands.

"I think so. Do you still do gymnastics at that club?"

"Uh-huh, all year long. George, do you think if you're in training for competition, you should drink? Even a little?"

"I guess not. If you're on a team at Franklin and they catch you drunk, you get kicked off."

"I know. If they catch you."

"Mercy, I don't really drink beer."

"George—I figured that out already."

When she got home, Mercy found Ernie sitting alone at the kitchen table. "You're back early? Everybody else in bed?"

"Yep. 'Specially Fred."

"The dance was so strange. Hey, what's the matter?"

"Huh?" Ernie twirled a ballpoint pen with his finger.

"Yeah, your face is blotchy and red. And how come your party got broken up?"

"Marylee and I got broken up. We had a fight."

"Oh. That's tough. Want to tell me about it?"

Ernie shook his head. As the pen twirled faster, it skidded across the table. Mercy caught it. "But listen, Ern, about what happened at our dance." Mercy told him about the "drunks." "That junk never happens at Franklin dances, right?"

Ernie gazed past his sister with puffy eyes. "Nobody pretends they're drunk at Franklin dances. Because they *are* drunk."

"Not the athletes!" Mercy snapped. "Fred never drinks!"

"He's always saving himself. Rest of 'ems not so pure."

"Do you mean like *you*?"

Ernie made a pistol of the ballpoint pen and pretended to shoot out the light fixture. "Too bright. Pow, pow."

Mercy glared at him. "You're not crying over breaking up with Marylee. You're just smashed! Dad would be so upset, Ernie!"

Ernie snorted. "Come on. Only one of us is so damn important around here. Not you. Not me. Gee, who's left?"

"O.K., so Fred's the big star. Dad would still have a fit! What if you have to go in for Fred or some other guy tomorrow, and you're hung over? Don't you even care?"

Ernie refused to answer.

"Mom and Dad are more interested in Fred now, sure. They're proud of him. And next year he's going to college. But that doesn't mean we can just blow off our lives, does it?"

Ernie mumbled, "Maybe. I'm just tired of waiting my turn."

When he lurched away from the table, he tipped his chair. Mercy grabbed his arm. "Dad will hear you. Come on, go to bed and sleep it off." She pulled him upstairs and shoved him into his bedroom.

Worn out, Mercy flopped onto her bed. You never could go to Flip City with a hangover. Nobody could fly from bar to bar, or hit the horse, or dance down the beam, without being in perfect control. The coaches would spot a kid getting into a bad habit.

But Ernie was getting into bad habits, and nobody was spotting it. In spite of what she said to Ernie, she wished her parents weren't quite so involved with Fred these days. Then maybe they'd see how tough it was to be living in his shadow.

Early Saturday morning Dina awoke to a series of sounds she'd heard twice before that week: Mom in the bathroom running the tap, trying to cover the sound of vomiting. She sat in bed, listened and re-membered. This week she'd come home with Rose and Theresa from school, only to find Mom asleep on the couch. Dina had seen these symptoms before. Her mother had been pregnant twice since Theresa was born, once after Anthony was killed. Dina knew all about the sick stomachs and exhaustion, and later the trips to the hospital when the babies came too soon for their tiny lungs to keep breathing.

This time Dina prayed the pregnancy would work. Before, Mom was still grieving for Anthony and had worked too hard to forget. Now Dina at thirteen could ride herd on her sisters, and they could all help with housework. Mom would just have to rest. Then Dina smiled to herself. First she'd better be certain that this wasn't just the flu!

She pulled on a sweatshirt and jeans, then went to the kitchen to await her mother. She started the coffeemaker and lined up the cereal boxes on the counter. As she sat and waited, she wondered how she could bring up the subject.

Rose and Theresa came down, already arguing over which cartoon came on first, and which girlfriend was coming over to play with whom. Dina tried to shush them. She'd have to get Mom to make her announcement in front of the three of them. As Dina set out three servings of cereal, Mom walked slowly through the door.

"I smelled the coffee. Thanks, Dina."

Dina poured her a mug. "Are you feeling O.K.? Kind of tired?"

"A little. I went to the doctor this week." Rose and Theresa stopped eating. "I wanted to be sure things were holding on. And guess what he said?"

"I know," Dina smiled.

Mom lightly patted her belly. "We'll be having a baby on April first. Hope he won't be such an April Fool."

"That's great! I know he'll be super!"

"The doctor said that as long as I rest a lot, things should go just fine. They have wonderful machines now that look inside at the baby and listen to what he's doing. Amazing."

Mom sipped her coffee. Dina could see that Mom was convinced this baby would be born at the right time. Dina thought, I'm going to see that it is.

Then Dina noticed a delivery truck backing into the driveway. "Mom, I think it's my practice beam," she said. Two men hauled a long parcel out of the back.

"Oh, I'm not dressed and your father's still shaving. Dina, show them where to put it."

Dina ran to open the rear hatchway to the basement playroom. She'd almost forgotten this big event of the day. Her parents had painted and carpeted the downstairs room for her. No excuses, Pop had said. You walk that beam every spare minute. And Dina knew he was right. The more slow-paced time she spent doing tricks, the better prepared she'd be for the tension of competition on a high beam.

Mom, Rose, and Theresa came down to watch Dina unwrap the beam. Theresa asked, "Can I play on it sometimes? Can you show me tricks?"

"I guess. But you have to be careful and know what you're doing. Even on a low beam."

"Yeah," Rose said. "I saw Dina's friend Von fall off the beam and she almost split her head open."

"Dina, did she?" Mom asked in a flash of panic.

"She did *not*." Dina snapped at Rose. "She just slipped and hurt her neck a little. She's practically fine now."

"You can get hurt playing soccer," Rose retorted. "Ellen Lacey got kicked in the ankle and slipped, and she has a cast on now."

"Oh girls, please!" Mom protested. "Don't upset my stomach." She pointed at the younger girls. "This beam's for Dina to work on. Not for horsing around!"

"Mom, this beam is only four inches above the ground," Rose said in hopes Mom would relent.

"So? People have drowned in bathtubs with only four inches of water." Mom stopped. "Listen to us. We sound pretty silly."

At that moment, Pop ran down the stairs. "Nobody touches that beam yet. I have to be sure it's anchored in the standards. This floor isn't completely level."

As the commotion swirled around her, Dina got her usual slightly removed feeling. When everyone talked at once, she wondered how she could be part of this family. But eventually the novelty of the beam wore off. Pop made some sales calls, Mom went shopping, and Rose and Theresa's pals raced outside to play. Dina spent the day with four baskets of clothes in the basement laundry, her portable radio, and her beam. As she tried handstand after handstand, getting the feel of this new wood in this new place, she day-dreamed about having as many friends as her outgoing sisters. They always seemed to find girls their age living nearby. But Dina sensed she'd never be able to handle the pressure of a large social group anyway. The gym team usually gave her all the socializing she wanted. Gymnasts liked and respected her because she worked out hard and performed well. They didn't care how cool or sharp she was. But now, she admitted to herself, having just a *few* friends at school would make a difference.

That afternoon while Dina stood at the refrigerator pouring juice for herself and six small back-yard athletes, the phone rang. "Dina?" A familiar voice! "It's me, Sue."

"Oh, hi, Sue."

"Hi. What's happening?"

"Not too much. I'm watching my little sisters. And I got this new beam delivered today."

"Really? A beam in your house?"

Dina knew that Sue was never too sure what one did on gymnastic apparatus, or why Dina was always doing it.

"It's a practice balance beam down in our basement playroom. What are you doing this weekend?"

"Life is boring, as usual. But next Saturday, my mom said I could have a sleepover. My sister's going away, so we can have extra room. Can you come?"

"A sleepover?" Dina's heart thumped as if she'd just completed a backflip dismount. "That would be great." She scanned the kitchen calendar. "Next Saturday?" The date read: "Dina, 2PM Meet at Jacobsen's." Oh no, what time would they get home?

Sue continued, "I figured I'd call you and Alicia and Kelly Ann and Sara J. We'd have pizza about seven, mess around, you know. So I'll see you?"

"Yes, but I don't know how early. I have this gym meet out of town. You can't tell how late they'll run. Maybe you could save me a slice or two? I'll hurry."

"No problem. Just don't get totally tired, because we'll probably stay up half the night talking."

"I won't." Dina grinned while rising up and down on her toes. "Should I bring anything?"

"If I think of something, I'll tell you at school."

* * *

After she hung up, Dina skipped down the stairs and hopped onto her beam. Powered by her excitement, she did a series of leaps down its length, then without any apprehension, flipped into two back walkovers. A sleepover, a sleepover, she chanted. She sat down slowly on the beam and folded her arms. For the first time in years, Dina resented the demands that gymnastics made on her life. For once, she had someplace else as wonderful to go.

Jules was spending Saturday afternoon on her slant board in the billiard room, lifting hand weights. She heard Evalene's footsteps overhead in the pantry, where she was putting away the week's supplies. As Jules popped her favorite U2 CD into her player, she stretched, flexed, and daydreamed. She loved the dim solitude of the billiard room, a hiding-place where she could ignore the pile of homework on her desk: a list of French verbs and idioms, a novel to finish, a chapter of math problems to solve. She fantasized about the coming meet, where she'd amaze Joe and her teammates by winning bars and floor. Then she remembered Dina was competing, although she'd already qualified for States in the previous meet. So she imagined she'd take *second* place, which would still impress the team. She too would qualify, and everyone would be proud.

After twenty-five sets of every lift she could do, Jules hauled her sweaty aching body to her feet. She heard the sound of high heels above her. Mother was home from her meeting.

"Julia? Come up here, please."

Jules couldn't miss the displeasure in her mother's tone. Now what had she forgotten to do? Slowly she climbed the stairs and found her mother standing by the kitchen counter with the day's mail spread out. Although Evalene busied herself in the pantry, Jules could sense that she was listening.

"What did you want?" Jules asked. "I was working out."

"Aren't you invited to a party tonight?"

"Just Trevor's birthday, no big event. About eight of us."

"Parties are as important as your gymnastics. And what about your hair? You promised to get a cut today."

"Oh, sure. I still have time. Mr. Rick said he could take me right after four."

"Then get yourself together. You never leave yourself enough time to get to these places. And one more question. When did we sign permission for you to go on the French cultural excursion to Montreal?"

Kate Wolcott held out the Winchester School student-faculty newspaper, which was mailed to all parents. The French cultural excursion was the headline story.

"Mother, I told you," Jules said. "I can't go to Montreal, because the trip is over Thanksgiving break."

"We'll miss you at Thanksgiving dinner. But this kind of trip will broaden your horizens. Surely you can still sign up?"

"I can't go! We have a Sectional on that weekend,

that qualifies you for States. I gave Daddy that schedule a month ago when they announced it at Flip City.
Didn't he . . ."

"Julia, what are you talking about? A gym meet?
And you don't even know if you'll be in this Sectional?
Correct?"

"I know I'll make it. I just have to." Jules heard a
defensive whine enter her voice. Lately any conversation with Mother ended in confrontation.

"I'm furious that you're refusing this trip." Mother
glared at Jules. "A chance to improve your French,
impress your teachers, which you certainly need to
do. We send you to Winchester for a reason. It's not
just a place to pass your time between gym meets."

"Yes, but Daddy thinks my responsibility to the
team is important too." Jules started backing out of
the kitchen before she exploded. "He says that sports
can teach you to hold up your end. . . ."

"Your father will say that education comes first!"

"Yes, but Mother . . . my haircut." Jules bit her lip.

"Oh, run and clean up. Evalene can drive you."

Jules dashed up to her room and made it into the
shower before she started to cry. Why couldn't she
ever live up to what Mother expected? Why couldn't
she get her point of view across? Later, as she dried
off, her tears slowed. She figured she was about to
have one of her erratic periods. Maybe that explained
the bumps on her nose and the sleepy spells she had
yesterday in class. She wondered if Mother had ever
been troubled by bouncing hormones.

As she fixed her hair, she muttered at the image in
the mirror, "No trim is going to help. It's hopeless.

And what's the good of going on the French Cultural Excursion when I'm doing so badly in the stupid class?" The failure in French wouldn't come home until mid-term, about Thanksgiving. Jules prayed that the grades wouldn't be delivered until after the Sectional, so she'd have some victory ribbons to clutch and display. But even ribbons wouldn't help Mother understand what Flip City meant to her.

As Jules passed the study, she saw her mother with her feet propped up on a hassock, sipping a drink. "I'm leaving for the beauty shop," she called, trying to get out.

"Do you know where your father is?"

Jules frowned. It was almost four. Obviously Daddy had not yet told Mother about his weekend workouts. Jules felt like a fool lying for him. "I don't know, Mother. I need money for Mr. Rick."

"Oh. Grab a twenty from my purse in the kitchen."

At last Jules was safe in the car, where she grumbled to Evalene, "I don't know why I can't talk to Mother. We just blow up. Doesn't she think I'd like to go on the French trip? It's probably going to be fun, even though I wouldn't be able to say three words. But I can't just dump Flip City! I have a commitment to the team. The French trip is optional. Scoring well at the Sectional means States for me."

"Just say to Mother like you did to me."

"I can't. She makes me crazy. I thought Daddy explained it all to her. Don't they talk to each other?"

Evalene squinted at the avenue and made no comment.

"So," Jules continued, "could you talk to Mother for

me? You go to the meets, you know how I get a lot
out of the team."

"Can't talk for you," Evalene replied. "Like we said
about going to this boarding school, you got to get
strong. Stand on your two feet. That's what Mother
wants."

"But gymnastics is making me strong! Can't she see
that?"

"You settle things between you," Evalene said. "I
only work here, Jewel."

Jules felt a sharp stab from that reply. She had always taken Evalene's support for granted but lately
she seemed to be pushing her away.

Evalene pulled up in front of the beauty shop. "Listen. Maybe this year is the last one for a lot of things.
Last year for you at Winchester, maybe last year for
us to be together so much. You follow your mother
now. She needs you."

Mother? Needed her? Evalene obviously knew
more than she was telling, but Jules wanted her to be
on her side, not on her mother's. "All Mother *needs*,"
Jules decided, "is for me to get prettier and smarter,
so I can be a big hit at boarding school. Which is never
going to happen."

"Stop feeling sorry for yourself. Take one day at a
time. Now worry about hair. And what clothes to wear
for Trevor's party."

"It's just a few kids, no dress-up deal."

"Still. Ask Mother about what to wear."

"Oh. I get it." Jules adjusted her retainer, hoping
she wouldn't mumble for Mr. Rick. "Taking Mother's
advice cheers her up."

Evalene winked. "That's it, Little Jewel."

As Jules hurried into the beauty shop, she thought about the party. She hoped it would be fun. But why couldn't Mother understand that Flip City was even better than a party? There Jules could take out her retainer, let her hair fly, and just be herself.

Von dressed in her crisp white blouse and black waitress skirt Saturday morning. Friday had been a fantastic day. Her English teacher said the first draft of her personal essay on "The Meaning of Minority" looked so promising she wanted Von to polish it for a contest. And at Flip City, not only was Mercy back in competition, but Von had performed five perfect beam exercises in a row, actually causing Eileen to applaud. At dinner when Von had described her rebound in gym, Mother had been pleased. But Father wanted to hear about academic success. Von and Mother reminded him that achievement in sports could help girls get grants from colleges, a fact he found unbelievable. Still, he agreed to keep paying the gym tuition as long as Von kept up her high grades. Her elder sisters said Father was getting soft, too liberal with his youngest. To herself Von promised, "Just watch and wait, I'll do it all!"

Rummaging through the kitchen, Von found that the bread drawer was almost empty. Her brothers had eaten the last of the Portuguese rolls. She loved the fat chewy ones with crispy twists on each end. She decided she'd run over to the Vasquez Bakery on the corner and buy a fresh bag when she got her break from busing tables at the Saigon Café.

After she finished her breakfast, Von went downstairs to the store where she found Mother organizing stock and Father making entries in the inventory books. Since it was nearly ten, they'd open the store soon. "Hello lazy girl," Mother smiled.

"I won't be late," Von replied. "All I have to do is set up the tables before eleven. Plenty of time."

"Today is the biggest day," Mother reminded her. "You work fast, help your sisters." Then she said louder for Father's benefit, "Eight hours of work. Good thing you are so strong from Flip City."

Von chuckled. "That's me, girl of many muscles."

Father came over to give parting advice. "Remember, do what the customers ask. But always follow the instructions of your brothers-in-law. They are the managers."

"Yes, Father."

"Also make sure they feed you a good dinner before the evening crowd," Father said. "Keep up all those muscles."

Von nodded. Father could be sort of sweet. She grabbed her coat and rushed out the door.

When the clock struck three that day, the staff at the Saigon Café took their dinner break. Von sat at the back table with her sisters and their husbands, wolfing down whatever she could stack on a plate. She was starving after watching people eat for four straight hours. Her sisters teased her about eating so much that she'd put them out of business. Von noticed that her eldest sister was picking at her food, yet swelling beneath the apron. She must be expecting a child at last! Von knew that when they had to pay a replacement waitress, that salary would greatly reduce their profits. Even so, her family would be so delighted to have this grandchild. They'd all find a way to help out.

"I have to buy some things," Von said as she left the table. "I'll be back to do the setups for dinner."

Her sisters agreed, so Von walked briskly the few blocks to the Portuguese bakery. Her tips jingled in her apron pocket. Although she knew Mother would reimburse her for anything she spent on baked goods, she decided she'd buy a few of those rolls just for herself.

When she entered the nearly-empty bakery, she didn't see any of her favorite item. With a frown, she surveyed all the glass cases so closely she hardly paid attention to a teenaged boy with a handsome mop of black curls who was leaning over the counter. "What can I get you?" he asked.

Von looked up abruptly. The boy spoke without the Portuguese accent of the owners, but he resembled the family. She told him, "I need a dozen rolls."

The boy grinned. "Don't I see you working down at the Saigon Café sometimes?"

"That's me. My family owns it."

"Oh. They serving Portuguese rolls now?"

"Come on," she smiled in return. "They're for me. I'm hooked on them. Please don't be sold out?"

"A girl with great taste." The boy reached under the counter and pulled out a bag. "Here's your fix for the week. Our last dozen. Now what else?"

"Oh, a white bread. And are those new cookies?"

"I just invented them. Better try a couple fast!"

Von laughed as the boy forced cookies into her

hands. "Do they let you give away the goods in here?"

"Sure, they're stuck with me. I'm the boss's nephew. Hey, did I see you on the bus to Bush?"

"Um-hum." She munched, enjoying the cookies.

"I'm new here this year. My mother and I moved up from New London. Bush is a great school. So, you go there?"

"I'm a freshman," Von admitted, knowing she looked younger.

"Thought so." He studied her openly.

Von started to feel self-conscious. She'd never really flirted much with boys, and now that she had the chance, she was afraid to carry through. So she stared at the cookie trays. The boy wrapped her purchases, then rang up the register. "That's six-fifty. My name's Riccio. What's yours?"

"Von." She was too nervous to eat her last cookie.

"Von? So, how late do you work? I could walk you home?"

Von was delightfully unsettled by his offer. Although her parents considered her to be too young really to date, she'd always socialized in groups with the Vietnamese boys they approved of. The idea of this guy showing up at the café for her, even for something as innocent as a walk home, was shocking. As she held out the money to pay, Von glanced up at Riccio and thought, "He's so good looking."

No way would her brothers-in-law let her walk off with Riccio, a stranger to them. She had to stall, and hope she could still keep Riccio's interest. "One of my big brothers always comes to take me home," she told him. "Father makes him. I'm the youngest, so they all treat me like a kid."

"Oh sure." Riccio shrugged off the rejection. "Guess maybe you're too young for a guy like me . . ."

"Well, I have to get back to work." Von thought that sounded very mature. Then as she backed towards the bakery door, she flashed a perfect smile. "If we meet on the bus, you could sit by me."

Riccio beamed in return. "All right!"

Dancing down the pavement, Von skipped over the cracks, swinging her bag of baked treats. Suddenly "having it all" didn't just mean making the Honor Roll and Class III States. It meant having a boyfriend. But in spite of her pounding heart and excited spirit, Von knew she'd never get Mother to go along with her on this one. Boyfriends were the biggest taboo. Still, she could hope.

6

Thirty at Jake's
October 22

Mercy felt like a racehorse waiting to burst through the gate. With her weight down and her skills up, she planned to make a fresh start at today's meet at Jacobsen's. She even worked with Mom to create a new sleeker hairdo. When the Dibellas came for her, Mercy tossed her bag across the back seat and greeted them happily.

Dina turned and beamed at Mercy. "Your hair looks super!"

"Thanks. Mom did the French braids and double ponies, and I trimmed the bangs. Think it makes me look more professional?"

"Yes," Dina replied. "You look like you're on the Olympic team."

Mercy chuckled. "Wait until you see Jacobsen's Gym. It's a long way from those fancy field houses where they have the Olympics. It's the top floor of an old building, and it echoes like a cave. No spectators' gallery—parents all crowd along the sides."

"Don't worry," Mr. Dibella told Dina. "I'll be down front."

"And you have to do your floor routine around these two pillars."

"Are you kidding?" Dina asked Mercy hopefully.

"Nope. But we get used to them in warmups. Everybody gets the same handicap. And wait until you see the runway to the horse. It runs along this wall of mirrors—guess it was a dance studio once. You can see yourself running out of the corner of your eye!"

"Oh. Well, we won't let it shake us," Dina said tensely.

"Sure. Oh, my folks said thanks for taking me today. They have to go to my brothers' football game at Franklin. Some college scouts are talking to Fred. They'll drive to the next meet."

"Tell your parents you're welcome to ride with us any time," Mr. Dibella said. "Dina's the number one athlete in our house. I'll be driving to all her meets."

Dina wished she could find the chance to tell Mercy, "If my brother Anthony was alive, he'd get scouted and Pop would be watching him. So don't think I'm so lucky and wonderful." But she knew she didn't have the nerve to say it out loud.

At Jacobsen's, they were soon drawn into the flow of girls and their families climbing the stair to the cavernous old hall-turned-gym. Mercy spotted Jules's new shorter brunette haircut through the crowd.

"There goes Jules," she told Dina. "Last year when we competed here, she tripped on her beam dismount and fell into this fat guy's lap. He was sitting on the edge of the mat."

"They let them on the mat?" Dina asked, amazed.

"Sometimes it happens," Mercy said. "Jake's too

easy-going. But his apparatus is all regulation. And with the crowding, the judges take pity on you."

"Well, we're all going to qualify today," Dina said. "I know it. I mean, I feel it."

When Mercy flashed a huge hopeful grin, Dina sensed that her friend believed her vision would prove true. Unfortunately, Dina did not feel too well. Sporadically her lower abdomen seemed to contract, then throb with discomfort. She didn't have a fever or flu symptoms. Must be nerves, she thought. She pressed her lips together tightly, ignoring the pain.

In the crowded locker-room, they both spotted Jules, who was wedged in a corner pulling on her stretch pants.

"Hi Jules. You look tough today. Pumping that iron has paid off."

"And look how slim you are!" Jules returned. "Love your new French braids."

"Thanks. Hey, you've had your hair cut."

"Yeah, what do you think? He gave me this razor cut to establish height. I said, I'm tall enough! I bet it'll look nasty when I start sweating."

Von hustled over to add her opinion. "I told her, it looks super. No barrettes or ribbons to lose doing tricks, right? And she looks a year younger, more like the competition."

Mercy grinned at Von, who was self-conscious about being the oldest. "Did you see that T-shirt that says, 'As I got older I got better'? That should be our uniform."

"No thanks!" Von said as she rolled her shoulders and stretched her neck muscles.

"How's the injury?" Jules asked.

"It's fine. I did a lot of exercises, and I'm going to cruise today. Mother is here, watching me like a hawk. She has this notion I'm really going to get injured some time. Then it's bye-bye Flip City."

Mercy shrugged. "I never think about it, even though I've done both ankles."

"My brothers' Tai Chi instructor says the trick is to flow like the wind." Von raised on her toes, but failed in the packed room to move very gracefully.

Dina stood nearby, transfixed by the conversation. Von had reset her mind to *succeed* in spite of a bad fall, something Dina longed to learn how to do. Jules also had a physical problem with her developing height, but she didn't give up gym. She just concentrated on getting stronger. And Mercy kept the weight off, although for her it was a constant struggle. Dina didn't see herself as truly dedicated, compared to these girls. Even though she wanted desperately to score well, she wondered if she'd have the strength of character to overcome her own obstacles.

A fist banged on the locker room door. "Hey in there! All gymnasts out for warmups." It was "Jake" Jacobsen.

"You go on," Dina told Mercy. "I have to check the john."

So the Flip City girls filed over to Joe on the rear of the packed spring floor. Mercy pointed toward the wall. "Jules, is that Evalene with Mrs. Nguyen?"

"Yep. We came together."

Von sighed. "I told her, Mother, you may have to stand all afternoon. Jake's got no gallery. But she said,

'I stand in the store. So I'll see how good you do.' "

Jules sympathized. "My mother still isn't keen on gymnastics, unless the exercise improves my brain a whole lot."

The younger gymnasts clustered around Mercy and Dina, awaiting their rotation assignments. Loretta complained, "There are people all over the mats again."

"So it's crowded, no big deal." Mercy calmed her down. "The Gymnettes train here, and they win plenty of ribbons." She smiled at the girls, admired their slick ponytails, their "Lucky Bears" and other charms. "You just keep your mind on winning for Flip City, O.K.?"

Loretta and Amy danced with enthusiasm. Giggling, they flipped into impromptu handstands. Mercy recalled that at the last meet, when she'd been assistant to Joe, she'd planned to ignore distractions and stay focused when she was back in competition. But somehow she couldn't ignore the others' need for advice and reassurance, even though she was now their competitor. Good thing gymnastics was a sport where nobody got "benched," so long as they had the moves.

Joe announced, "This is how we go: floor, vault, bars, beam. Dina, this time you won't get stuck being last."

As Dina nodded, a look of confusion colored her face. Mercy noted Dina's peculiar expression. She gave her shoulder a pat, walking her over to start warmups. "No sweat for you today. You've qualified. So you can cheer for the rest of us."

"I will," Dina said soberly. "Everybody's going to score thirty. I can just feel it."

"Don't know where you're getting this secret information," Mercy said. "But I love it."

When the meet commenced, Dina discovered she was first from her rotation on floor, first to perform a precision routine around those ugly pillars. Taking a deep breath, Dina focused her attention on the obstacles. Thoughts of Pop, teammates, judges, coaches, were gone. Dina vowed to beat the pillars at their own game.

Mercy watched Dina fly through her routine, with the only noticeable breaks on her forward dive-roll. As Dina hit the spring floor, she had trouble pulling out. Mercy saw her bite her lip as she finished her final set of poses. As Dina dropped beside her, trembling, Mercy said, "What's wrong? I bet you beat your old score."

Dina gulped down a spasm and drew her knees up to ease her cramps. "I'm O.K." While the next competitor performed, Joe stooped and gave her a few criticisms. As the girl's exercise ended, Dina's score was flashed: "An 8.9!" Joe beamed. "Way to start the day!"

Dina smiled, receiving hugs from the team. Then she tried hard to be the cheerleader in turn. "Go on, you can do it too. Use those dumb pillars. Figure where you'll hit the floor and use them like guideposts."

Mercy, Von, and Jules were surprised to hear shy Dina come up with such aggressive advice. As Jules removed her stretch pants, she vowed to close in on Dina's incredible opening score. She would play the same head games and make her dispute with Mother worthwhile by qualifying for Sectionals.

The strategy worked. Jules scored an 8.1, and Von a 7.9, both excellent scores for them. Then Mercy rose to take her turn. When she saw Dina glued to her every move, sending good vibrations, she strode onto the floor with Dina's confidence in her own heart. She sucked in her belly, extended her chest, lifted her chin. She felt lean, poised for a fast start. Although Jake's gym became a noisy echo chamber jammed with shuffling bodies, Mercy never let the diversion register. She poured her energy into working those pillars, leaping, spinning, rolling in the precise spots. Her routine was over before she could believe it.

As the team waited through a Gymnette's routine, Joe congratulated Mercy. "Good job. You really psyched out those posts."

"It was Dina's plan," Mercy smiled.

When the score flashed, Mercy's eyes widened with joy. "An 8.45? That's my best ever!" She turned to Dina. "We are on a *roll*! You were right about using the pillars. Now what's the idea for the wall of mirrors along the runway?"

Dina rose with the group, as the rotation ended. She replied, "Mirrors? Who sees any mirrors? When the sun shines through those big windows at Flip City, the beams come down, but all you see is the horse. Do it the same here."

Von, who loved mind games, gave Dina the challenge. "You just show us how, all right?"

The younger girls vaulted, trying to practice Dina's focused vision. When Dina herself took her turn, she inhaled deeply, then saluted. Again, her abdomen rippled with pain. Gasping, she leaned over in a crouch, leveled her gaze past the shining mirrors to the horse. Give me strength, she prayed, and ran.

After she soared through her handspring, Dina hit the mat hard in a solid stance. The terrific jar of her landing sent a hot bolt through her torso. She summoned all her willpower to arch and give the salute that concluded her vault. As she walked back along the runway, she caught her own reflection: a shaken, slumping girl. Finally she admitted that something was wrong with her. When Joe came over to give her corrections, he told her the score looked pretty promising. "Then please, tell the judges I'm not going to take my second vault. I don't feel well. I've got to go to the bathroom."

Joe frowned. "Did you get hurt?"

"No. Just a little sick."

"Go on. I'll settle it with the judges."

Dina vanished before the other girls could talk to her. She thanked God the bathroom was empty, and locked herself inside.

Von, Jules, and Mercy tried to ignore Dina's departure and concentrate on vaulting. As Dina predicted, the team scored well. Mercy kept glancing at the bathroom door. Finally some Gymnettes lined up outside and knocked. The door remained shut. Mercy couldn't stand the suspense. "You know Dina," she said to the other girls. "She gets nervous attacks. I'll go give her a pep talk. She'll get it together."

"I could use a trip myself," Von said.

"And I need to rinse my lenses," Jules added.

Joe told them: "O.K., go get Dina, but hurry it up. The beam routines are slowing the rotation. But it's ending soon."

"We'll listen for Jake's announcement on the mike," Mercy promised. Picking their way through the massive crowd, the three girls made it to the bathroom. Mercy knocked on the door, then shouted into the crack, "Dina, it's me with Von and Jules."

After a long pause, the door opened. Dina admitted the girls, then slammed the door in the face of the Gymnettes. Dina's eyes were puffy, her lips tightly drawn. "Dina, you pulled an 8.0 on that vault." Mercy said. "And we all made the same, just like you said. We're all *cruising*."

"And your big event's coming up," Jules said. "You'll win bars for sure. So let's go."

Dina stared at the floor, forcing the words out in spurts. "I can't. Spots. On my trunks. You know."

Von and Jules met Mercy's surprised glance. Tiny Dina got hit today with her period? What bad timing. The girls nodded, agreeing to treat Dina's dilemma with a positive approach.

"So it's the first time, huh?" Mercy asked.

Dina's look of humiliation answered her question.

"O.K., so you joined the club. Take it easy. We'll fix you up." As she looked around the sad little toilet in vain for a pad-dispenser, she realized her own gym bag was empty. She asked Jules and Von, "You got anything?"

"Sure," Jules said. "I've got plenty. I'll go get my bag."

"I've got aspirins," Von added. "In the locker."

Von and Jules dashed out of the bathroom, ignoring the complaints of the line of gymnasts waiting a turn.

Mercy gave Dina a pat. "Hey, you'll be O.K."

Dina sank into a crouch, leaned against a trash can, and slumped her head onto her arms.

"So you got a few cramps? Bad place to get it, but it's exciting too. Everybody remembers their first time. I was on the school ground last year playing touch football with my brothers and some friends. There I went, all over my shorts. What was I going to say to my dumb brothers? I made up some excuse, biked home, and had to find Mom's pads. What a zoo! Mom really laughed, because it never happens at a convenient time."

Dina finally spoke. "Don't want it."

"It's nothing, Dina."

"Everybody will know."

"Huh? Not with the thin pads they have now. They even have athletes doing the ads."

"They will. Boys will know."

Mercy put her hand on Dina's arm, wondering what to say to someone who had such weird ideas. Boys never thought about that stuff. At least Fred and Ernie didn't treat her any differently. She looked at the scummy sink and overflowing trashcan. Then she thought about Fred on this fall afternoon, using muscle and wit to race a football over a line. Mercy could be there too, yelling the cheers, getting some reflected glory. Instead, she was sitting in a shabby bathroom trying to comfort a girl she barely knew. "Maybe I'm nuts," she thought. But Dina was on her team; and Mercy was a team player.

Jules and Von returned, holding out their offerings to Dina.

"Take this in the stall," Jules told her.

"And take these two aspirins," Von said. "You'll feel O.K."

"Do it quick," Mercy added, "because Joe is going to start yelling. I just heard Jake announce the last rotation."

"I can't do bars. You all go."

"Huh?" Mercy was losing her patience. "Dina, you can do that bars routine with two broken legs and still beat my score."

Fists started pounding on the door. A Gymnette called, "The rotation is over, and we have to *go*. Like *now!*"

"In a second," Mercy called back. She grasped Dina under the elbow and pulled her up. "We're going to win this meet. Together. Let's do it."

"I'm messed up," Dina whispered. "I'm scared."

"Scared of what?" Mercy demanded. "Getting your period doesn't change anything. You're still the best!"

"I'm not ready. I hate this stuff. You can get pregnant."

The girls stared in confusion. Mercy's sense of humor got the better of her. "Well, not on the bars, Dina. Maybe on floor, but not on bars."

An awkward silence fell among the girls. Would Dina pull out of this depression and smile? Suddenly a male voice said, "Dina, it's Joe! If you're sick, I have to see you."

"Just another second?" Dina pleaded with the girls.

"Joe, she's doing O.K.," Mercy shouted.

"It's me," Jules lied. "I dropped a contact, and we're on the floor looking for it. Nobody can leave."

"Oh terrific! Find it fast and I'll get the judges to give you a few more minutes. Hurry, or we forfeit."

Dina gave a wobbly smile. "Thanks."

Von formed a cup out of paper towels. "Quick, swallow the aspirins."

"You've got the team psyched," Jules said. "You can't back out now. You have to get yourself psyched."

Dina gulped the pills and took the pad. She gazed from face to face, and saw her team needed her. She had to invent a new head game, for this. Let's see, she'd call it "use the anger." Having her body out of control infuriated her. She ducked into the stall and pressed the pad onto her trunks. "Maybe it's a freak one?" she thought. "If I work extra hard, it might go away."

After yanking up her leo, Dina burst out and said, "I've got it together. Let's go for it."

Mercy grinned. "That's the way."

The four girls rushed over to the bars, where their rotation was underway. Within minutes, Dina found herself on deck. Grimly she shook out her limbs, inhaled and screwed on a smile. And she talked to herself. "Get mad, get tough." Then in an echo from her past, she heard her brother's voice in her head. "Teeny-Deeny, get up in the peach tree and fly!"

That was it! That's why she loved the bars best.

Flying was what she did with Anthony, when they used to play trapeze artists in the back yard. She'd never made the conscious connection before. She saluted: and she flew.

Mercy held her breath as Dina smashed her belly across the bar for the beats. Would she make it without breaking? When Dina rose from her dismount, Mercy, Jules, and Von gave such a shriek of relief that the whole floor of gymnasts turned to stare. They knew that Dina hadn't performed her greatest exercise. Too many form breaks and slips in timing marred its perfection. But she'd conquered her fear with her mind game and made it through.

Mercy felt so proud of Dina that she forgot her own intense bars anxiety. All she wanted to do was complete her own routine and be there beside Dina. So of course Mercy's exercise was the smoothest of her entire career.

Joe leaned over Mercy, grinning. "First you hide out in the john forever, then you run over and skyrocket through the bars. How come you don't do that every time? You kids will make me crazy!"

Mercy laughed, stunned by her own accomplishment. Where had it come from? The extra workouts with her brothers, the dropped weight? Her determination to show her coaches she was a winner? Or concentrating on Dina's troubles rather than her own?

After the bars scores were flashed, the girls were on fire. Even Mercy had scored a 7.8, by far her personal best. "We just have to make it through beam," Mercy said, "and we can score thirty all-around. We'll qualify!"

Von the mathematician ran some tabulations and agreed. "We can do it." She glanced over at her mother. "I want to show my parents."

Jules caught Von's meaning. "I'd better qualify too. Otherwise I'll never hear the end of it from Mother."

Dina stared straight ahead at the beam in silence. Her brother's voice no longer sounded in her mind, challenging her to make a game of it. On the beam, Dina was alone.

As several Flyers and Gymnettes preceded them in the rotation, Mercy stretched. "I wish this meet was over. It'll take forever to tabulate all the awards. It's so late now. . . ."

Dina's head snapped around. "Late?" She remembered that today was a memorable one for several reasons. "I have a sleepover. Mercy, can we grab our awards and run for the car? I'm never going to get there."

"Sure," Mercy answered, pleased to hear that shy Dina had some social plans. "Where's the sleepover?"

"Oh, this girl Sue from my gym class," she explained. Then Loretta poked her to remind her she was on deck.

Like a shot Dina leaped up, pulled off her warmups, and faced the beam. Although the aspirin helped, she felt jumpy, achy, fearful. Pulling a decent beam score meant everything to Mercy, Jules, and Von. Dina had to show them how to do it. Since they'd stood by her, she would stand by them. Besides, the sooner they finished this beam rotation, the sooner she'd get to Sue's, where she just might talk about this milestone day. And with her mind totally directed away from failure, she stayed centered, balanced. While she still had hesitations, she didn't slip once.

When Von's turn came, she used her own set of images and became a panther prowling a limb, flowing like the wind. The Beam Queen returned and conquered. As she flipped into a perfect dismount, Von knew she was back where she belonged. She scanned the cheering crowd. Somehow her short but determined mother had wiggled her way to the front. But Loan Nguyen didn't cheer or clap. She merely smiled with relief.

As for Jules, she heard Evalene's words in her head as she walked the beam. "Get strong. Stand on own two feet." Which is just what she did. As she saw Evalene wave the V-sign, she knew they'd both have the pleasure of telling Mother she was going to the Thanksgiving Sectional.

Driving home in the Dibellas' car, Mercy whispered to Dina, "How do you feel now?"

"Better. I won't have to miss the sleepover."

"Sure. You'll be fine. See you Monday."

As Mercy emerged from the car in her driveway, she saw streamers fluttering from the trees. Victory banners decorated the house. A sign taped to the car door read, FRANKLIN RULES. The students had demonstrated to Fred their spirit and admiration. No visible badges of victory awaited Mercy. Who cares, she thought; we won anyway.

In the front hall, Paul Samuels was shouting into the phone, "That's right, Dad, three colleges! Good schools, ones we could never afford. Oh, he's got to take these national tests. Yes, soon. Hey, here's Mercy. Want to talk to her?"

Dad handed over the phone. "Hi Gramps. I just got back from a gymnastic meet downstate."

"So how did you do, Sunshine?" her grandfather asked.

"Great. I made a high enough score to get me into the Sectional meet at Thanksgiving. If I do well there, I go on to the State meet in January. I'm working real hard at that."

"You don't get hurt doing that stuff, do you?"

"No," Mercy assured him. "It's safe if you do what your coaches tell you." She knew her grandparents were of a generation who worried about a female who did athletics. "Say, why don't you and Gram come if I make the State meet? I know it's not as thrilling as Fred winning a football game. But it's indoors where it's warm. You could see what *I* do for a change."

"January, huh? Not too much doing on the farm then. Guess we could pay a man to feed the stock. All right, Sunshine, we'll drive over, providing we don't get a blizzard."

"Providing," Mercy grinned. "Talk to you later, Gramps."

Mercy entered the kitchen, where Fred and his huge teammates lounged, filling the room. His girl-friend Caren gazed up with awe at his face. "Hi guys," Mercy said. Showing her wristful of ribbons, she added, "I made my thirty all-around."

"*All right!* Super!" Fred said. "Next meet, I'm coming."

"If it's not the same day as a game." Mercy

shrugged. "What's this about three colleges making offers?"

"Some coaches are going to try and get me a deal. They're from Division Two schools, which means heavy traffic for a guy like me. And they have to see my SAT scores before they can make any offers. When I took them last spring, I bombed bad on the math."

"You did?" Mercy said. "Get Ernie to tutor you. Where is he?"

A silence fell upon the athletes in the kitchen.

"He screwed up, huh? Don't tell me. He opened his mouth?"

Fred nodded. "He got suspended for a game or two. I can't figure him. He's *looking* for trouble."

Mercy touched her ribbons, then thought of the banners out front. Being an unnoticed victor like herself sure beat being a public screwup. She could not understand why Ernie was getting so messed up.

"Mercy," Dad called. "Telephone."

She ran to the front hall and picked it up. "Mercy? It's George."

"Hi George, I just got home this minute from the meet."

"I wondered if you're still going to Deb's party?"

"Sure, I want to go."

"My dad is driving me, so I thought, maybe you'd like me to pick you up. We could go together. Sort of."

Mercy smiled. George was trying to act mature to make up for his pep dance performance. She was starting to like him a lot. "That would be cool. Can you give me twenty minutes to change?"

"Sure. We'll be by at eight-thirty. Did you win today?"

Mercy didn't want to explain over the phone that they were all winners at Flip City. Any girl who got up and did what they did and bettered her score and helped her teammates was a winner. And if George didn't understand that, then he'd never understand Mercy. "Yeah, I won," she told him. "I'll see you soon."

7

Family Dinner

November 13

After weeks of struggling at school and at the gym, Mercy awoke one Sunday morning and decided she wasn't getting up. All week she had craved foods she shouldn't eat and had been exhausted. Part of her trouble, she knew, was the frustrating obstacle of mastering new optional tricks at gym. She could *see* herself performing the tough tumbling run and nailing the twisting vault. She could *see* herself making the cast handstand on the bar. But her body wasn't cooperating. Each time she started that tumbling run with a roundoff-back handspring, then pushed off for a layout with a twist, she almost made it around—but never quite all the way. "Take it on the backside!" Eileen had yelled, and Mercy had. She had bruises on her bruises.

The sound of chill rain spattering her window sent Mercy burrowing deeper beneath her quilt. Never had she felt so burned out. Finally Mom checked to see why she wasn't ready for church. Mercy complained about real pains in her lower back and overall achiness.

"I just can't get up, Mom. You know I hardly ever miss. Give me a break. I'll pray twice as hard next week. . . ."

"You've been killing yourself at Flip City," Mom decided. "Now you've come down with some germ. Well, stay in bed."

Mercy sighed, grateful to Mom and God. Of course, she knew she didn't have a serious injury or real germ. She'd come down with the Virus of Life. Her depression had begun Monday night when Eileen lectured her.

"Holidays are coming," Eileen warned, intimating that Thanksgiving stuffing and Christmas cookies could ruin you faster than cocaine. "If you don't lose more weight you'll never get your full front flip, or that twisting layout," she added, then concluded, "and the bars routine will do you in." Mercy clenched her fists, hiding the new rips on her palms, while Eileen insisted: "You can do it, Mercy. Just remember, no pain, no *lose*."

Reliving that weigh-in made Mercy even more depressed. She recalled seeing her teammates' worried faces when she left the office. They were afraid that she had been bumped again. The only person who looked equally unhappy was Dina, who'd been taken aside for a lecture from Joe. Mercy couldn't pry a word from Dina, but she suspected that Joe had given Dina the news from Marion about emotional disruption at meets. He probably said she'd better grow up in the nerves department, or she'd never be the top performer she had the potential to become.

* * *

Mercy's week had gone downhill. She struggled to master the new tricks, monitored each mouthful she ate. Still she slipped, fell, ripped, and flopped. Always hungry, weary, irritable, she lost her temper and snapped at her family. Her friends were steering clear of her. The final downer arrived Friday: a poor progress report in Math. Her first. Dad in his usual quiet but severe manner said she'd better get together with a tutor—maybe Ernie would do—and bring the grade up. Or else.

While her family attended church, Mercy curled up with her knees to her stomach and meditated on her condition. She'd lost her motivation to write her American History report or finish reading *My Ántonia*, things that usually interested her. As for her Spanish exercises, she couldn't care less. And what of her own future as an athlete? Was her goal of qualifying for the state meet unobtainable? She gazed at her windowsill where the four scraggly tomato seedlings she was growing as a science experiment struggled for life. Since she'd neglected to fertilize or water them, they slouched like injured athletes. Poor tomatoes, she thought, losers like me. Self-pity could surely take you right down to the pits!

As the clock neared noon, Mercy pulled herself together. Unless she was at death's door her family would expect her to be sociable, since Sunday dinner was often the only meal all five shared. Stripped for a shower, she decided this was the moment to step on the scale. If she saw the needle drop the smallest bit, she could eat family dinner with good humor. She placed her feet on the cold plastic pad. She'd been dieting religiously but the needle quivered, then stuck on the same plateau.

Muttering a few gross words, Mercy turned on the shower and let its hot spray wash away her anger.

As the family settled in their chairs for dinner, Mercy's eyes wandered across the dining room table: fried chicken, mashed potatoes, gravy, homemade biscuits, brussels sprouts drenched in butter sauce, jello salad with cream cheese topping. She couldn't eat any of it!

The family tore into their favorite foods. Trying to stay calm, Mercy told herself the Samuelses were large-boned people, men over six feet, who burned their calories easily. Mom at five-eight never dieted, although she never snacked either. Only Mercy was cursed with a stubborn metabolism and hungry fat cells. And sometimes Mom ignored her need for special food.

Silently frustrated, Mercy picked at her chicken, nibbled a roll, drained the butter off the brussels sprouts. After a while she'd consumed her small portions. She watched the others chatter while they refilled their plates, scraping the serving bowls. Mom turned to her and said, "Still not feeling good? You sure aren't yourself today."

That broke the dam. Mercy shouted, "I *am* myself. I'm not like you. That's the trouble. I can't eat all this stuff. Excuse me while I go peel a carrot!"

"Cut it out, Mercy," Dad said. "Athletes have to

eat! Do you want us all to starve? What's wrong with one decent meal?"

Mercy snapped at her mother, "*You* know what I have to eat. Why don't you fix it for me?"

"That's not fair," Mom replied. "I do fix things for you. But on Sunday I enjoy giving your father and the boys the things they like. They need to keep up their strength."

Mercy was angry. "If I had diabetes or some horrible allergy, you'd worry about what I ate. Keeping my weight down is just as important."

"There's nothing wrong with your weight!" Dad interrupted, an ominous note of warning in his voice. "If this gymnastics is going to make you rude to your mother, or ruin your schoolwork, then you'll have to find something else to do. Go on, fix what you want."

Mercy had been dismissed. She stormed through the swinging door into the kitchen and stood before the refrigerator feeling like a fool. After she found a hunk of cheese and a container of carrot sticks, she had to force bites down her tightening throat. She'd never felt so jealous of Fred and Ernie as she did at that moment. They ate like kings. But her needs were ignored, and she was yelled at. At times like this, she detested them.

Later that afternoon, Mercy came down to the living room where Dad and Ernie sat slouched on the couch, feet upon the oak coffee table, watching pro football. Ernie was scribbling notes from his history text while shooting glances at the screen. Mercy plopped on the floor beside them.

"Ern, I just talked to Chrissie. She's coming over tonight for tutoring at seven." Ernie had been helping Mercy's friend since her math grades had slipped earlier that year.

"Uh-huh." Ernie's eyes flipped between the TV and the page.

"So Ern, I have to sit in with you guys."

"Yeah? How come?"

"Because I suck at math."

"Since when?"

"Since I got a poor progress report."

Ernie's eyes turned to his sister. "Who have you got?"

"Budinsky."

"He's still alive? I had him in seventh."

"He hates me. He talks to me like I'm a retarded insect."

Ernie grinned. "Yeah, he probably does. But you were great in math last year. What happened?"

"Math got harder. And Budinsky's the worst. I can't follow anything he puts on the board. He tells these dumb stories, and my mind wanders."

Dad looked up from the football game. "Maybe last year you weren't so beat every night before you did your homework?"

To Mercy's surprise, Ernie took up her cause. "No, it's Budinsky. Mercy, haven't you figured him out yet? He doesn't like big-mouthed girls."

"Oh thanks. I thought you were on my side."

"I am. He doesn't think girls have a future in math. He's just an old fart who wants girls to write down the right answers and go away. You keep asking him to make sensible explanations, right? Maybe you talk to some kid next to you to stay awake?"

"Maybe."

"Well, cool that. We'll learn math at home. It's easy. You just have to shut up in class and give the right answers."

"I guess. Chrissie's doing better already."

"Because I'm a master tutor. Hey, Chrissie's dad even sends me some cash for my efforts. Maybe your dad would, uh, renegotiate with me?"

Paul Samuels looked at his son, whom he had grounded for breaking training and getting suspended. "You do a good job for your sister, and we'll talk about some kind of settlement."

Mercy smiled at Ernie, hoping the two of them could help redeem each other.

By seven Mercy sat beside Chrissie at the kitchen table, listening to Ernie expound on percents, fractions, and decimals. He wasn't above using bad jokes, homespun explanations, silly diagrams, even chopped-up apples for visual examples. Mercy realized that Ernie saw math as common sense, not the abstract mystery of the ages. Ernie took his talent for granted, while Fred sat upstairs pounding his forehead over the SAT math. Maybe everyone had some skill that the others envied? What was *her* special quality? She remembered something Fred had once said about her: "You do the most with what you've got."

Perhaps that was it. She did not give up, not at the gym nor in class nor with her friends. She watched

Ernie check her problems, then hand back the paper. "Keep at it," he said. "You're doing better already."

"I won't quit," she assured him. "We have to hang in, Ern, even if we still end up center bench."

"Speak for yourself," Ernie mumbled.

"I do. Hey, are you done with explaining division of fractions?"

"Sure. You both got it right."

"My supper was pathetic. Can I eat the apple quarters?"

Dina and her father handled Sunday dinner: broth with orzo, roast chicken, and greens. Mom had come down with respiratory flu. Pop assured the girls that all Mom had was a low-grade bug, and she'd soon be fine. Rose and Theresa believed it and went on playing their rainy-day games. Dina, however, couldn't help feeling anxious as she listened to her mother cough and gasp.

Unintentionally Dina took her nervous irritation out on her sisters. She criticized their behavior at the table, and later picked on the way they loaded the dishwasher. Finally Mom, tissue box in one hand, mug of tea in the other, gave some orders.

"Rose, will you please read to Theresa until her TV show comes on? I need some peace! Here, read a few chapters of her *Charlotte's Web.*"

"Dina reads better," Theresa protested.

"Rose reads fine. I want to see Dina in my room for a talk. Rose, dolly, do as I ask." Dina, feeling embarrassed, followed Mom upstairs.

* * *

Mom stretched out on her rumpled bed and sipped her tea, and Dina sat on the edge. "How are you feeling?" Mom asked her.

"Me? Fine. I'm hardly ever sick."

"I know, thank God. I meant, did you get another period?"

Slightly embarrassed, Dina shook her head.

"They may not be regular at first, but soon they will. You're starting to put on muscle and get tall."

"Mom, tall in our family means anything over five feet."

"Bet you're past that now. Go look in my bottom left dresser drawer." Dina obeyed. "Take out those sweaters. They were small on me last year, and I know I won't be able to get into them after the baby comes. You try them on, if you like them."

Dina yanked off her sweatshirt and slipped into a long red wool one. It was excellent! As she modeled for her mother, she said happily, "This is really cool, with the oversized look."

Mom smiled. "Only a few weeks and you'll be an official teenager. Might as well dress like one."

Dina posed in front of the mirror and gazed at her reflection. She didn't look like a kid in her mom's clothes, she actually looked like a teen. Well, a petite one. The experience was unsettling but exciting.

"Are you getting along at your new gym?" Mom asked. "You seemed very upset last Friday night."

Dina frowned. "The new optional tricks are hard. Tough moves on floor and bars. Joe and Eileen are riding me."

"You're a great gymnast," her mother said softly. "You learn new tricks in no time. Is this the same trouble you had in Albany?"

Dina nodded. "Joe lectured me. About getting too nervous at meets. He's kind of mad about that." As Dina relived the humiliation, her cheeks burned.

"I told you a hundred times, don't worry so much!"

As Dina tried on a navy wool sweater with a Fair Isle patterned neck, she asked, "Can I wear this one to school tomorrow?"

"Sure, they're yours. What do you have to do this evening?"

"I wanted to watch this national competition on the cable sports network. But I know Rose and Theresa want to see Disney."

"Let's do this: send the girls up here when the show comes on. We can get Disney on my little set. Then you'll have the den."

"Mom, they'll bounce all over your bed, and . . ."

"They're just kids, dolly. Think I'm not used to kids? Go tell them. And stop talking like I'm falling apart."

Arms filled with sweaters, Dina smiled and headed for her room. As she put her gifts away, she planned to wear the navy with her best stone-washed jeans. Before she laid the chosen sweater out for tomorrow, she held it up to her and gazed in her mirror: it *did* make her look thirteen. Maybe having her body "fill out" a little wasn't so terrible.

As Dina hurried down to the den, she heard Rose finish reading her chapter of *Charlotte* for Theresa.

"Rose," she said, "Mom wants you two to watch Disney up on her set with her."

After the girls trudged off, Dina tuned in the meet. As she watched girls not much older than herself spinning through the air and landing solidly with a smile, she did her series of conditioning exercises and timed handstands. Then Dina saw a gymnast do a difficult bars dismount, one similar to Shelley Steiner's. Only this girl did not over-rotate and break her ankle. Shelley was the rare exception, and nothing so bad would ever happen to Dina—or so she told herself. She would never break form or concentration, and she would *never* get hurt.

As she lay back she folded her hands on her belly, and felt a familiar burning sensation. "It" was back. Then the phone rang. "Hey, Dina?" the voice said. "It's Mercy."

No longer shy with Mercy, Dina talked freely about the meet, her mother's flu, the gift of sweaters, working on optional tricks.

"I know Eileen's pushing you hard on beam," Mercy said. "But it's paying off."

"Thanks, but I still hate it. I wish I could just compete the other three events."

"Me, too," Mercy agreed. "If I could dump the bars, I'd be a star. Well, a minor twinkle. But you've got the stuff, Dina."

"Joe isn't so sure." She decided to confess her shameful lecture. "I wanted to curl up and die. Now I know how you feel. After a weigh-in."

"We'd all be perfect if we could," Mercy said. "It

gets worse for me. I got a poor progress report in math from Budinsky."

"You did? I have him too. He's so mean, I can't stand him!"

Dina was proud that Mercy was confiding in her. Mercy's problems were almost as bad as her own. Maybe, she thought, she could learn from Mercy how to be steady and strong. But if they got *too* close, Dina might have to tell Mercy the whole truth about her past. And she was in no way ready to do that.

The Wolcott family hurried from the Buick to the back entry, dodging raindrops as they returned from church. When her parents and grandparents entered the kitchen and shook off their coats, Jules moved beside Evalene who was bent over the large oven. Jules inhaled deeply. "Mmm, smells like your Bavarian Feast," she said.

Evalene nodded, basting the crown of pork roast.

"We are starving," Grandfather announced, as he took away the coats. "And chilled to the bone. I believe we'll have coffee with our meal, Evalene."

"Yes sir, warm you right up."

"I'll warm up with a drink." Kate Wolcott filled a glass with ice, then headed for the liquor closet.

"Terrific," MacArthur Wolcott said critically, "when we've just come from church."

"Yes, where the heating system was poor and so was the sermon." Kate winked at her daughter Julia, including her in this rebellion. "From now on, I think I'll have a drink before we go!"

Jules didn't know whether to giggle or not at her mother's irreverence. No one else smiled. Rather than have them stand around and watch Kate drink, Grandfather ushered the group into the dining room. Evalene set out all the hot dishes. "That be all?" she asked Grandfather.

"Yes, we'll help ourselves now. Have a nice day, Evalene."

The housekeeper departed to her quarters, since the rest of Sundays were "off" for her. Either she did her personal shopping or stayed closeted with her TV to watch sports. No one bothered her under any circumstances.

"Actually," Grandfather said after Evalene left. "I believe I too could use a glass of wine. Keep the blood flowing. Alice? MacArthur? A bit of rhine or sherry?"

"Yes, sherry," said Grandmother. Jules was surprised, since her grandmother almost never drank except at parties. Grandfather served her.

Jules never did understand how the fighting began. Oh, no one screamed or threw anything. But understated vicious arguing began between her father and mother. Many things surfaced that Jules had only suspected—her mother's discontent with her father's constant absences on business or time spent at clubs, her father's anger that her mother couldn't take charge of important community committees, accusations on both sides about secret activities, and ugly disagreements about Julia's priorities with academics and gymnastics. At this point, Grandfather stood up. "That's enough, both of you! After you've been married nearly twenty years, I can't understand how you have failed to solve any of these difficulties! And Julia should never have to listen!"

"That's right!" Jules jumped up. "I'm not listening to any of this!" She ran from the dining room into the kitchen, then found herself drawn down the back hall. She ended up standing in front of Evalene's door, trembling, still in shock from what she'd heard at the table. Never had she wanted more to knock on a door. She heard the sounds of the sports announcer, sounds of Evalene moving around, probably cleaning up her quarters. At last she couldn't endure it—she banged her fist on the door.

Evalene flew to the door. "What is it? Fire?"

Jules started to swell with tears as she grabbed for Evalene's hand. "They're all fighting! It's horrible and I can't stand it."

Evalene drew back her hand and folded her arms. "I'm sorry. But I can't take you in, Jewel. Bad things hiding in this house for a long time, so maybe now they have to come out. But you go back. I can't be your family now. No good any more for us."

Jules winced as if she had been slapped. "What?" she whispered.

"God, don't look at me like that. I can't come between you and your parents. You just get into worse trouble. You got to stand on own feet, get things right for yourself. You see?"

"I don't see . . . what everybody wants from me?"

Evalene's composure broke and she gave Jules a long hug. Then she took Jules's chin in her hand firmly. "I got my own family in Poland, and we got trouble too. Only way I keep going is to get strong and make it on my own. Best thing I can teach you, my girl. Best way to love you. Now go back down to your people."

Jules suddenly understood what Evalene had been doing with her all this fall. She was trying to break her dependence and send her to Mother, even if it hurt both of them. It was painful, but Jules felt she had to respect Evalene's judgment. She wiped her eyes and kept her chin up as if she were walking onto the floor at a meet. As she passed into the front foyer, voices still echoed from the dining room, where Grandfather was trying to mediate. Then Jules peeked into the paneled den, Grandmother's hideaway. In a large leather chair Grandmother sat alone, holding the remote control, randomly switching channels on the TV. When she saw Jules, she hit the off button and said:

"Come in Julia, and shut the door."

Jules did so, then sat in the other leather armchair.

"They're still arguing in the dining room," Jules said.

"I know. We're in for a rocky time around here. I don't know where all this anger came from. But it isn't our affair, Julia."

"I know some of it has to do with me. I'm not making Mother very happy. I mean, she thinks I'm sort of a flop."

"Julia, you can't make up for the problems in anyone else's life. You're only a girl. I think you are wonderful."

"Thanks." Hearing that did make Jules feel better.

"Let's play cards," Grandmother suggested. She pulled a deck out of the drum table between their chairs. "It will pass the time until things settle down out there."

Jules remembered playing gin on Sunday afternoons with Grandmother when she was little. It seemed like a century since they had really talked except at the dinner table. Jules dealt the hands and heard the rain patter on the leaded windows beside the fireplace. As they played cards, Grandmother said, "So, dear, tell me what you're doing at Flip City so far this season? I haven't kept up with your progress."

Jules realized that since her mother wouldn't permit her to discuss gymnastics during meals her grandmother was left out. So she tried to explain about her optional tricks on bars, the beautiful new floor music, how pleased Joe had been with her performance at Jake's, how good it felt to be a winner. She even talked about her dreams of making it to the State Compulsories, and of being on the winning all-around team and bringing home the trophy. Grandmother kept nodding, making comments. Jules then mentioned some of her teammates' problems and how they were trying to help each other overcome them. Grandmother told Jules: "I want you to continue with your gymnastics as long as you can tolerate the activity, and you still love it. If this team makes you feel proud of yourself, then you will keep going. No matter what happens between your parents. I can't drive anymore, but I will pay the tuition and hire you a driver if they complain. Even though I never pursued my dream, you shall have a chance at yours."

Jules looked up from her cards in surprise. "What dream? You wanted to be a gymnast?"

"No, I didn't even know about female gymnasts when I was young. I wanted to be an equestrian."

"You did? I never knew you liked horses."

"I adored them, especially mine. We had a house in the country, and I begged my father to have a champion riding horse. I dreamed of riding in competitions. My father was against it. Proper young ladies didn't hang around barns and compete on teams with men for ribbons. Now even an English princess does it. But my mother feared for my safety, since it was a dangerous sport. So I never trained for competitions. I rode at home and behaved myself." Grandmother discarded. "Gin."

"I can't believe you were a rider! What happened to your horse?"

"Why, he grew old and died. When I married Franklin, I moved here to his family home. Julia, I probably wouldn't have won a single competition. I wasn't that strong. But just once I wanted to try. Oh, don't look so sad. Far worse things can happen than losing a girlhood dream. Just take yours as far as it will go—and win your next award for me."

"I'll try. My only chance is for a place on floor; if you make the top ten in your class, you get a gold medal. If by some miracle I win it—it can be for both of us."

Grandmother laid down her cards and patted Jules's hand.

Suddenly the huge house seemed to shake. Someone had slammed the front door.

* * *

As Von reached up to the top shelf for bowls, her shoulders and upper arms throbbed. She tried not to wince, so Mother wouldn't notice. At Flip City this week, the timed handstands and the new swinging moves on the bars had caused Von to overstrain her muscles. But Mother had complimented her after the meet at Jake's, pleased she'd qualified for Sectionals. And Mother's pride was keeping her going to the gym. So she refused to let her pain show.

As she set the large oval kitchen table, crowding in the eleven place settings, Von heard her aunt and uncle arrive. "Go greet them" Mother said. "Sister and I will finish the table."

Von did as she was told. Her aunt and uncle liked to fuss over her. They brought her ice cream, her favorite treat, and always asked about her progress in school, so Father could brag about her. Von knew her father had great love and respect for the older brother who had sponsored the family's entrance into America. So Von too was glad to see them and tried to impress them by saying the correct things.

After hugging them and accepting their tub of Breyer's chocolate chip, Von sat beside them on the sofa and inquired after their married children. As always with her elders, Von spoke Vietnamese.

"How is your gymnastic study coming along?" Von's aunt asked, hoping to bolster family enthusiasm for Von's athletics.

"Pretty well, Aunt. I won some prizes at a meet a few weeks ago." Von pulled her ribbons off the shelf. They never looked too impressive when held up against the breakfront laden with soccer trophies. Since both brothers were soccer stars, they received tuition grants from City College; now the older brother made money by officiating at matches. But Von's aunt praised her nevertheless for her reds and golds.

"I'm going to try for the blue on beam at our Sectional meet," she told her aunt. "My routine is perfect now. Our team is so strong this year, most of us will go to the State meet."

"Ah. And what could you win there?"

"The top ten in each event win a gold medal. If my team wins with the highest total score, we get a huge trophy for our gym."

"Very interesting," said her uncle, who thought that gymnastics were an unlikely vehicle for future success. "And how are you liking high school?"

"I'm doing fine, Uncle."

"There are some rough boys at that school," her uncle warned. "We hope you stay with boys you know and trust."

Von nodded. She saw her brother Hai glance over at her. Hai knew about her special relationship with Riccio. Von said, "My classes are with very good students. Nobody bothers me."

"Good. Has your first set of marks come yet?"

"Our teachers told us last Friday."

Her uncle grinned with confidence at Von. Her father also stood beaming. Mother rested in the doorway, wiping her hands, waiting. The rest of the family watched Von. She swallowed.

"In English: A."

"Ah." Everyone smiled. Von's English was superior.

"In French: A."

"Ah." Her father had been the only one to master French in Vietnam, and he was eager to see Von master it also.

"In math: A."

"Ah." Expected by all, since Von did math effortlessly.

Von spoke the next part so fast, her syllables bumped into each other: "In science, B, in chorus, B, in health, A."

A silence. Father asked: "What was that? Bs?"

"Science is so difficult, Father. We have to learn about a hundred kinds of rocks, and I get confused."

"Rocks?" Father and the family looked to Hai for confirmation, since he had done well in science.

"She has the hardest teacher," Hai said. "But she can do better. I'll help her, and by end of term, she'll make an A."

"And what was that other one?" Father asked.

"Chorus," Von whispered, thinking, Here it comes, hiding the truth, which I do so badly.

"But Von," her aunt said. "You sing so wonderfully. At Saint Anne's School you had the solo parts. How can this new teacher not love your singing?"

"I don't know, Aunt," Von said and avoided her eyes.

"I can't understand," Father added. "The sisters said you had a good voice. Maybe you sing too quiet at the high school?"

Von looked down at her hands. "Maybe."

Hai interrupted. "Mother, is dinner ready?"

"Oh, yes!" Loan's small fingers flew to her lips.

"Come to the table, before I burn it all. My daughter will be furious after she spent all morning cooking."

The family crowded around the table, happy to be close and well fed. Von was ignored as the conversation turned to other areas of family concerns. After the meal, Von and Hai took turns washing and putting away dishes. They spoke in rapid low-pitched English, their usual trick to keep their parents from understanding much if they overheard.

"I know why your grade in chorus got dropped," Hai said. "Josie figured it out."

Von sighed. She'd forgotten that Josie, a senior soprano, was one of Hai's girlfriends. "What did she say?"

"That you cut too many times in one quarter, so they dropped you a grade. Better stop that crap *now*."

"What else did Josie tell you?"

"How you have chorus after lunch, so you just kind of hang around the cafeteria, till the monitors don't notice and the next shift comes, and you can sit with that Spanish guy."

"He's Portuguese," Von snapped.

"So what? You're just a kid. You'll get in trouble."

"Hai, how can you say that? Riccio is a nice guy! He's just lonely, because he's new here. I feel sorry for him."

"Oh, yeah? You need better friends. Father will lock you in your room until college if he finds you going with any boyfriend, let alone one who isn't Vietnamese. And somebody around here may tell him."

"Come on, give me a break."

"Not me. Somebody in the neighborhood. People

will see him walking with you. He's not your class, Von. You can be the best student at Horace Bushnell High. The best. But you have to keep your head straight and your attitude right."

"What makes you think Riccio is so bad?" Von persisted.

"Come on. He's a hunk. What does he do, anyway?"

"He plays soccer and has a part-time job. Just like you."

Hai was surprised into silence.

"See? He's not so bad. I won't cut chorus anymore. Please, let's just forget it."

Hai lifted stacks of dried dishes onto the high shelf. "You don't remember how it was in our country, Von. I can still remember. I'm telling you, stick with kids who remember. Because others just dump you in the end. I know, Von."

Von, deep in her heart, faced the truth: Hai was becoming biased against people who were not Asian. He felt it was O.K. to play on a soccer team with them, or go to school with them, but never to get really involved with them. Well, Von decided, I'll never feel that way about Riccio or Jules, or anybody. "Don't worry about me. I won't forget our culture," she told Hai. "I have Vietnamese friends, I go to their parties, I go to temple with Mother on holidays. But nobody is going to tell me I can't go with anyone I want."

"You're trying to hang around with those rich girls at gym," Hai said. "You think their families are going to let you in? They think you're cute, but that's all, baby." Hai left Von to finish cleaning the counters.

As she worked, Von wondered sadly what had happened to change Hai. She knew there was plenty of subtle prejudice against Asians. She'd just been lucky so far not to suffer from it. Abruptly she was startled by the phone's ring. She sprinted for it, wondering if it might be Riccio, who had teased her, threatening to call her at home. "Hello?" she said quickly.

"Hi Von? It's Jules. Can you talk?"

"Hi Jules. Sure, what's happening."

"Some pretty bad news."

"Oh. Tell me." Von could picture it: Jules had failed a subject, and her mother was making her drop out of Flip City.

"It's my parents. Something set them off at dinner today. And they argued all afternoon. I ran out of the room, but I think it was like a dam breaking, and all the bad stuff poured out. My grandfather tried to settle it. But my father finally left. And my mother locked herself in her bedroom."

Von didn't know what to say. The situation sounded nasty. "Jules, take it easy. You'll be O.K. Maybe they just need to see a counselor or something."

"I don't know. I feel like a jerk, tiptoeing around my own house, hiding in the den with Grandmother. I'm going to explode from all the tension."

"You better come to workout tomorrow," Von advised, "and get it all out on the apparatus. You'll feel better."

Jules felt tears well up again. "I will." But she didn't think she'd feel better for a long, long time. "So, what's happening at your house?" she asked, hoping Von would do the talking while she steadied her voice.

Von told Jules in soft phrases about her family dinner, her grades, her brother knowing about Riccio, all the while sneaking peeks at her family clustered in the living room. She saw her father leading a discussion. And she wondered about the Wolcotts. Whatever was going on, Von knew Jules was going to suffer.

Jules listened avidly to Von's story. She'd carpooled with Von for three years, yet had never been to visit her apartment. Von said she was welcome; but the Wolcotts never found it "convenient" for Jules. Now Jules liked Von's story better than her own. Although the Nguyens' place might be crowded, poorly furnished, in a modest section of town, Jules wished with all her heart she was sitting in it now.

8

Thanksgiving Sectional

November 25

"Is this the place?" Fred said, pointing to a monstrous old brick building which looked like Dickens' idea of a reformatory.

"Yeah, home base for the Marvelles. I remember it from last year," Mercy replied. As Dina, Fred and Ernie followed her up the stairs they were greeted by the racket made by five teams of gymnasts with their coaches and families. Mercy pointed.

"See the goodie table?" she asked her brothers. "You can go munch out and kill an hour while we warm up."

"All right," Fred agreed, "but we still want the best seats on the bleachers. Let's dump the coats and save some space."

"Not right down front," Mercy said. "I don't want to see your faces inches from my dismount mat."

"Aw." Ernie looked crushed. "Your biggest fans?"

"Yeah," Fred said. "We wore our letter sweaters to impress all your girlfriends, and you want to stick us in the cheap seats."

Dina giggled. Mercy's brothers were cute. Even

Mercy suppressed a grin, as she told them, "O.K., we're all snowed. You can sit in the middle."

"Now you girls get out there and kick butt," Ernie said.

"He means good luck," Fred amended for Dina, who melted into a blush.

Inside the changing room, Mercy and Dina encountered Jules and Von, along with their younger teammates who had qualified. Mercy sat beside Jules on a long oak bench. Jules slumped as she stared into a mirror.

"How are you doing?" Mercy asked.

Jules shrugged. "Not too great. Thanksgiving was a disaster. My father now lives in the guest room. He talked to my mother in *her* bedroom. He talked to my grandparents in the study. He even talked to Evalene in the pantry. As usual, none of them talked to me. Which is just as well, I guess. I just want to get through this meet and do O.K."

Mercy put her hand on Jules's shoulder but could not cheer her up. They'd all heard rumors about the situation at Jules's house. "Maybe you should get real mad, and use that energy," she said.

Jules kept staring into the mirror. "If only I didn't look so bad. My haircut grew out. Now it's hanging in my face. I've got about fifty zits from all the stress. And I cut my lip on my retainer."

Von leaned over Jules with her makeup kit and hairspray. "I told you, I break out every month. So what? Just cover them up. Want your confidence back? I'm your makeover lady."

"Von's right," Mercy agreed. "Looking good can

give you an edge. Even Loretta and Amy fuss over their hairdos."

As Von worked on Jules, Mercy studied her body in a leotard. In spite of the Samuels' Thanksgiving eating orgy, she'd managed to shave off one more crucial pound, holding her total loss at eleven. Eileen encouraged her, saying if she hit her goal of fifteen, she'd have a fighting chance at States. If she stayed in top condition. If she didn't incur the slightest injury. And if she got very lucky, and the downstate competition wasn't too tough. A lot of ifs—but Mercy wanted to believe.

Dina stood beside her, running a comb through her thick hair. Mercy asked, "How are you feeling today?"

"Really great," Dina said resolutely. "I'll show Joe what I can do when I get my mind set. I'm going to kick butt."

Mercy chuckled. Then she noticed Dina's head hit a bit higher on her shoulder. "Did you get taller lately?"

"An inch since September," Dina beamed, pleased that Mercy had noticed. She was in high gear, determined to perform well.

"Ladies!" Marva Decker, coach of the Marvelles, stuck her head in the door. "Out for warmups. Now! Hup, two!"

"That's Marva in action," Mercy told Dina. "She runs a meet like a marine drill instructor. The Marvelles like her a lot."

The girls marched around the cavernous gymnasium until they spotted Joe beside their team spaces on the bleachers. "Girls, keep those warmup uniforms on whenever you're not performing," Joe said. "The draft in this barn is fierce."

The girls warmed up on vault. Since the runway was laid out along the bleachers, they had a chance to search for familiar faces. Von nudged Mercy. "Who are those handsome hunks in Franklin High sweaters? Waving thumbs-up at you?"

"You know that's Fred and Ernie," she replied. "They were good sports about bringing us today. My folks *had* to go to this retirement banquet for the vice-president of my dad's company."

"Where's Mr. Dibella?" Von asked. "He never misses."

Dina overheard. "I made him take my little sister to her soccer match. It's the championship, and Rose is the youngest kid on her team. She gets jealous that he's always with me."

Von winked at Dina. "Don't tell me. You have another sports champ in the family?"

"Rose is very good," Dina said. "And she's tougher than me. If I had to kick and push my way through a meet, I'd never make it. She's got guts."

"It's so cool that your brothers came," Jules said to Mercy.

"Mine are always working or studying," Von said.

"Fred usually is too," Mercy said. "His football team made the state tournament, and he has to sweat the books so he can impress the colleges. But Dad made him take a break today."

Mercy saw Mrs. Nguyen perched on her stadium cushion, crocheting. "Guess your mom brought you and Jules?"

Jules jumped up to do her warmup run for the horse. But her coordination was off, and she overshot. Von whispered to Mercy, "You heard about the war at her house?"

"Some. Think her folks will work it out?"

"Who can tell? Jules can't figure it all out." Von stared with sympathetic eyes at her friend. "They always looked like the real American family, didn't they?"

After warmups, the teams lined up for their formal introduction and salute. As Marva Decker shouted the names over her mike, Mercy scanned the bleachers again. Her eyes traveled up to the huge windows near the rafters. A spooky rumbling rat-tat sound echoed. Rain or sleet? Then the recording of the national anthem and the cheers of the spectators drowned out the weather.

Only the best girls from each gym school had qualified for this meet. Joe told the team, "You'll have to earn every point here. So don't panic if your opening scores aren't as high as you've been seeing."

Mercy glanced at Dina's expression; but this pressure didn't appear to faze her. She looked determined, telling Amy and Loretta, "More competition is good. Everybody's at their best. So they push you to do even better."

The younger girls grinned at Dina, their new idol. As the meet progressed, they watched Dina prove her point, drawing energy from her opponents and concentrating on scoring higher. She blocked out the storm sounds, the new judges, the temptation to hide in the bathroom. The team applauded wildly after her floor exercise; her backflips and leaps were flawless. Von go so energized by the competition that she had to force herself to hold back. She kept telling herself, don't over-step, don't over-tumble, keep that control. And her self-discipline showed in her scores.

After the second rotation, all the Flip City girls had averaged between fifteen and sixteen, putting them in good position. Only Jules lagged behind with lower scores. Joe was aware that she had trouble at home and school, so he didn't ride her. Von and Mercy failed dismally in their attempt to keep her spirits up.

As the team moved across the gym to compete on bars, Von looked up at the bleachers to get her mother's smile of approval. She blinked, and stared. Someone had arrived unnoticed and sat beside Loan Nguyen, a pale thin woman wearing no makeup, a long Irish wool sweater, and jeans. Von hardly recognized Mrs. Wolcott. "Jules," she said. "Look over there."

Jules blinked to clear her lenses. "It's Mother!"

"How about that?" Von wondered if Jules was pleased.

"I can't believe it," Jules said. "How did she find me? And she just hates to drive in the rain."

"Well, she did it today," Von said.

Mercy also studied the mysterious Mrs. Wolcott who never attended meets. Today she didn't look too elegant. Then she glanced at Ernie and Fred, who were absorbed by keeping scores and talking about the opposing gymnasts. In the front row beneath them, a familiar couple marched in and sat down: an intense man with a notebook, and a damp disgruntled child in a soccer jersey. "Oh oh," Mercy said to Dina. "Looks like your sister's big match got rained out."

"Aw, poor Rose." Dina waved at her family. "She was so sure she was going to win."

"Better show 'em how. You're on deck for bars," Mercy said.

As Dina swung through her powerful routine, Mercy experienced her usual bars clutch. God, how she'd love to show her brothers that she too could come through for the team. If she could perform a solid exercise on bars with her brothers watching, she'd be forever grateful.

Waiting her turn, Mercy chalked her palms, praying one of her nastier calluses wouldn't rip. She bounced on the balls of her feet, shook the tension from her arms. And she ordered herself to "go for it!"

When her exercise was complete and her dismount executed without a flop, Mercy crumpled with relief. She had not been near Dina's level, but she had done a credible routine. After her score of 7.0 was flashed, her brothers figured her overall. Then Fred held up four fingers on one hand, four on the other. Mercy nodded. She needed an 8 on beam to be assured of a trip to States. If she stayed on and kept her timing, it was possible. She spoke to Von, whose scores were almost the same.

"We have to go for 8. You'll be O.K., you're the Beam Queen. But it's going to be a reach for me."

"It's all in the mind up there," Von said. "You can do it."

Mercy leaned over to Dina, who seemed to be in a

trance. "Hey, Dina, what's your head game for the beam?"

Dina rotated her shoulders. "Uh . . . you know, beam's my worst. I never think of it as up off the ground. It's a strip painted down the middle of this wide sidewalk. All I see is the strip. I try to feel it with my feet, then all the way up." Dina shrugged. "Doesn't always work."

"Sounds good to me. I'll try it," Mercy said.

"Who helps you come up with these games?" Von asked.

"I think about them, every night before I fall asleep."

Mercy exchanged glances with Von and Jules. They all had so many other things on their minds. Mercy thought about homework, her diet, her brothers, what she was going to wear or do with her hair, George Feder, somebody's party. But Dina sat beneath her gym posters and did conditioning and thought about her mind games. The girls watched Dina get up and focus on the beam. Would it all pay off for her?

This day the beam was hostile to Dina. She slipped off after a roll. She landed easily and hopped back up to finish. But the fall shook her focus. Her dismount was shaky. As she returned to the mat, she murmured, "Guess I blew it anyway."

"Not so bad," Mercy said. "And your overall's so high already that you'll qualify easily. I still have to do it."

"Think light," said Von, "and flow like the wind."

Mercy grinned, thinking that advice was cute from

Von, who weighed about ninety-nine pounds. Mercy then helped Joe set the springboard for her mount. She squinted her blue eyes and tried her best to see nothing but that strip down the sidewalk and to feel like a dancing feather. And for that moment, it worked!

After dismounting, Mercy gave the judges a proud salute, then flashed her eyes to her brothers. They shot their fists in the air and cheered. Then they watched Von perform one of her best exercises, moving fluidly and landing solidly after each spin and leap with grace. Her narrow feet held to the wood as if attracted by an unseen magnet. At the close of her exercise, Von spun to watch the score standard with Mercy's score.

Fred and Ernie led the shouts: A perfect 8!

"I did it!" Mercy hugged Dina, Von, and the team.

"Great going," Joe complimented her. Von also qualified, as of course did Dina. But Jules did not make the grade. Joe stooped beside her. "Not your best day. But we have two more Sectionals in December. You'll improve. You meet me in Marion's office before workout on Monday. We'll talk about things that might be slowing you down."

"Just you?" Jules asked. "Nobody else?"

Joe nodded. Jules agreed.

While they awaited the awards, Mercy said privately to Joe, "Did you see how cool Dina was today? She helped us all, and she didn't have to go once."

Joe smiled. "I'll be sure the Boss Lady knows about it."

Von was flying as high as Mercy. She'd shown her mother that they made a sound decision to stick with

Flip City. The state meet was in her future now. Her goal of getting into optional meets and making it through Class III had a solid reality. She wanted to celebrate and to show her friends her other life. She asked Dina, Mercy, and Jules, "Can you come and eat with us at my sisters' café? The food's real good."

Mercy called her brothers over. "Dad gave us money for dinner. So can we go to Von's family's restaurant?"

Ernie asked in a low voice, "What's Vietnamese food like?"

"Like Chinese, I guess. Von says its good. We can follow her mom's car. Come on, let's do it!" Mercy begged.

"Sure, I don't care," Fred said. "Are we bringing Dina?"

"You ask Mr. Dibella while I get our stuff." Mercy rushed toward the changing room to tell Dina the news. On the way, she bumped into a downcast Jules, standing beside her mother. Jules remembered her mother was a stranger to the team. "Mercy, this is my mother. Mother, this is Mercy Samuels."

"Hi, Mrs. Wolcott. Von asked us to meet at her sisters' café in the city for supper. Can you come too?"

Mercy gave Mrs. Wolcott her most engaging smile. Jules realized that her mother had made a real effort for her, having found the faraway meet and sat through the strain of competition and defeat. Now Jules was asking her to drive into the city and eat dinner in a restaurant where the only other adult in the group would be Mrs. Nguyen. Mother, she realized, had always gone out with Daddy on Saturday nights. Now she had few choices. . . . "I'd sort of like to go, Mother," Jules said.

"Then we'll do it. But we can't stay late. We have to talk this evening. Do you know how to get home from this place?"

"It's just down the street from Von's apartment. Evalene and I have driven there a thousand times."

"That's right," Mrs. Wolcott smiled. "Tell Von's mother to drive slowly. We'll follow her back."

As the Samuelses and Dina walked out of the Y to follow the Nguyens and Wolcotts, Fred nearly slipped on the steps. "It's freezing. Mercy, this weather rots. We'd better go home."

"Oh, come on, Fred. You can drive real slow."

"Yeah, but getting home later may be tough."

"We'll get good directions. Please don't back out?"

Fred looked at Ernie. They both shrugged. Maybe the sleet would let up later. They hated to ruin Mercy's big day.

The regular patrons of the Saigon Café gazed quizzically at the sight of four girls marching past in blue-and-gold team suits with colorful ribbons dangling from their wrists. Von's mother seated the group around the big corner table, then ordered what she knew these novices would like best: salads, crisply fried spring rolls, barbequed shrimps, beef strips, platters of rice-noodles. "My daughters also make good cheesecake," she said. "Everyone gets a piece for free."

Although the Nguyens used chopsticks, Von urged the rest to use forks and fingers. Dina, seated between her two large heroes, got so involved in eating that she forgot she was usually picky about new foods.

"You sure this stuff is dietetic?" Mercy asked Von.

"Sure, if you use chopsticks. Then you drop so much, you never gain a pound." Von winked at her mother.

Mercy tried a pair. "You're right!" She grabbed her fork.

"It's excellent, Von," Jules said. "May I have another piece of cheesecake?" She turned to her mother, who was sipping wine and smoking. "You only had some rolls."

"I had enough, dear. I didn't have such a strenuous day as you." Kate automatically brushed the bangs out of her daughter's eyes. "You order all you want."

Von called to her sisters in Vietnamese to bring more cheesecake and tea, then smiled at Jules. She sensed without knowing why that something sad was going to happen to Jules, and she wished she could keep her friend with her all night.

Soon Mrs. Wolcott rose to leave and insisted on placing a great deal of money on the table. Von could see Jules was upset, so she didn't protest—she just quietly said goodbye.

Kate Wolcott drove slowly, following Jules's directions. "I might as well tell you now," she said. "I've decided your father and I have to live apart for a time, to find out why we have so much trouble. But we must be the ones to leave. The house belongs to your grandparents and your father. The Wolcotts built it in 1870. I'll look for a nice condo for us, one nearby so you can carpool to Winchester and Flip City. Your father will make the down payment."

"Why can't I stay in the house?" Jules blurted out. "With them? With Evalene?"

"Your father has no time to be totally responsible for you," Mother insisted. "And Evalene is your grandparents' housekeeper. We'll take care of ourselves. We'll be fine."

Jules tried to picture Mother doing all the shopping and cooking and cleaning, things Mother had never done before. Then she pictured the two of them each evening, stuck with each other, when they hardly spoke now without disagreeing.

"You'll visit your grandparents every weekend," Mother continued. "During the week, we'll be very busy."

Jules had to say it. "Maybe you'll do better without me."

Kate pulled into the long driveway. She hung onto the wheel. "I can't do without you. I can get along without all the committees, Julia, but not without you. We have to make it together. Promise me you'll try."

Jules saw Mother bite her lip. *That* was the real reason she was making Jules move. Jules tried to say something kind, but the words stuck. Instead, she ran for the house.

Back at the Saigon Café, Dina, Mercy, and the boys ate until they were stuffed. Fred forgot the rotten weather and his plan to leave early. Ernie forgot he had a late date. Mercy and Dina laughed with the Nguyens over stories about their getting adjusted to

America. At last Mercy noticed the other diners had left. Von's sisters were leaning against the cashier's counter, smiling through their weariness. She peeked at the clock behind the paper lantern. "Fred, it's almost ten. I lost track."

"Is it? We have to go! Dad'll think we got lost."

"Thanks for coming," Von said. "It was super."

"The greatest," Mercy agreed. "See you Monday."

Von's brother-in-law emerged from the kitchen to give Fred directions. Fred then drove a few blocks from the café, and got confused. Ernie squinted through the streaked windshield. "Damn, this is a one-way. Take a left a few blocks down."

"No Fred," Mercy said from the back seat. "I saw a sign that said Cornwall Hills. That's not far from our neighborhood."

"Be quiet," Ernie said. "Fred, keep going left. I think we can hit Route 12 further on."

"No Ern," Mercy insisted. "We can take Bain Avenue from Cornwall Hills, can't we? By the cemetery?"

"Cool it! You'll get Fred all confused!"

"You sure about Route 12?" Fred asked. "I never went this way."

"Well, that guy at the café said so."

"Fred, don't get us lost!" Mercy said, feeling nervous.

"We're not lost!" Ernie shouted.

"Yeah? So where's this Route 12?"

Dina cowered in the corner. She had assumed the Samuelses were the most amiable, calm people she knew. Mercy leaned forward in her seatbelt, ready to argue further with Ernie. She opened her mouth. Her voice froze as she saw the windshield glisten beneath the wipers, then dissolve into a sheet of white blinding light. An oncoming van crossed the median and came straight for their hood. A scream stuck in Mercy's throat.

"Fred!" Ernie gasped as he threw his arm in front of his face. "Look out!"

Like a shot Mercy's strong right arm flew out as Mom's did when they were kids. As she smashed into the seat before her, her arm made a barrier that saved Dina.

Instinctively Fred avoided the head-on collision by pumping the brakes and swerving the wheel violently. Metal crunched and the glass shattered as the car jumped the curb and crashed into a utility pole. Mercy heard an explosion of sound—the last she remembered.

A long silence was broken by Dina's soft sobs. Ernie brushed off shards of glass, then turned in his seat. "Mercy?" He saw his sister slumped sideways in the dark. "Dina? What . . . ?"

"Her head," Dina cried. "Help her!"

Ernie turned to his brother. "Christ! Your legs are caught!"

"Get Mercy out," Fred said, spitting words between waves of pain. "Get cops. Ambulance. Can't move. Drive shaft."

Ernie reached over with his left hand and struggled with the door, since his right wrist was broken. He staggered around and opened Dina's door. She kept sobbing. Mercy lay across her, quite still. Suddenly they were surrounded by cars. A siren wailed.

9

Homework

First Week in December

After two days of being wheeled around the hospital, pumped with drugs and X-rayed from all angles, Mercy was sent home. The doctors told her she was lucky to have only a concussion and a dislocated jaw. Half her face looked like a bruised tomato, making chewing fairly agonizing. Murmuring as few words as necessary through clenched teeth, Mercy sipped her pureed meals, for which she had little appetite. She spent a week at home resting and worrying about Fred.

Several times Mercy told her parents the crash was not Fred's fault. They hushed her, saying they understood he'd been run off the road; avoiding the head-on collision as he did probably saved Ernie's life. But Mercy knew they didn't understand. She had insisted that Fred drive to the Saigon Café in freezing weather, kept him there late, quarreled with Ernie moments before the crash. The underlying fault was hers.

Fred, however, was not available to blame or absolve her. He lay in the hospital recovering from surgery on his knees. His football career was over. Too much damage to the bone and cartilage. Start back with swimming, then biking, but no contact sports. That's what Mercy heard Dad tell her grandparents on the phone. Ever since then, she'd eaten herself up, fearing Fred could never live without football.

Mercy talked to Ernie—but did not receive much comfort. With his hand and wrist set in a cast, not only was Ernie knocked out of football season, he was unable to do anything requiring his right hand. Each day he grew more temperamental than ever. Mercy asked him, "Do you think it was mostly my fault?"

"Don't be stupid."

"I mean because I pushed you into going to the café. . . ."

"Were *you* the idiot who ran us off the road, then didn't even turn back to see if we were dead?"

"No."

"Then don't talk crazy." Ernie was seated at the dining room table struggling to write the answers to his advanced algebra. "How can lefties do this?" he griped.

"I can copy it over for you," Mercy quickly offered. She bent over the tablet and her head started to throb. The doctor had predicted she'd get headaches for weeks. As she stifled her moans, Ernie became more irritated with her.

"Lie down and take your codeine," he told her. "Mom can do this stuff for me later."

"Ern . . . you don't think your wrist is ruined forever?"

Although the cuts on his face were healing, Ernie still resembled a boxer after a few rounds in the ring.

"All I'm missing is the state tournament game, where I'd never get my buns up off the bench. Big deal. And maybe I'll never play the violin, but I'm not ruined forever."

"You sure? It's healing?"

Ernie managed a wry grin. "We're all going to be fine and dandy, even Fred. Hey, you better be back in my math class on Sunday night when I tutor Chrissie. No slacking off, or you're sunk."

Mercy produced a wobbly grin of her own. "Thanks, Ern."

Most days Mercy lay in the den, enduring bouts of depression and self-pity. Time off from school, she discovered, was no party when you felt terrible and looked worse. She'd seldom been sick, and her injuries had allowed the use of walking casts. Never had she experienced such a dull recuperation. Only George Feder's visits gave her real amusement. His funny observations about teachers and kids at school, combined with a witty recitation of class notes, gave her a few smiles every day.

One evening after George had related his notes on the War of 1812, Mercy tried to start a serious conversation.

"We all went down to see Fred today."

"Yeah? Good. How's he doing?"

"He says the pain is better. But he's in these awful huge splints. He must figure his life will never be so great again, without contact sports. So, do you guess he hates me?"

"Huh? Hates you? I'm not following this."

Mercy sighed. "Forget it. Too complicated."

"O.K. So when are you going back to your gym?"

"My coaches, Joe and Eileen, call me every few days. They say come back as soon as my headaches are gone, so I can start stretches, pullups, easy stuff. Otherwise I'll stiffen up. They think I can get back in shape for Compulsory States. But I think it's hopeless."

"You can do it," George said. "You have until January."

"But can I get my momentum back? I just laze out now."

George gathered his books. "I think your head got rearranged with that concussion. I don't know you when you talk like that."

Mercy didn't always know herself these days.

Friday night, Mom called Mercy to the phone. "It's Marion."

"Marion?" Mercy answered, surprised.

A warm low-pitched voice greeted Mercy. "I talked to your mother. She'll bring you back to workout next Monday for a few hours, so we can see what you can do. All of us want to help you get going again. The team misses you a lot."

Mercy was touched by the quality in Marion's voice. She knew she was missed. Joe, Eileen, and Dina and the other kids who called her regularly told her that. The wacky get-well cards and notes told her that. But Marion's word made it official, special. "I miss Flip City," Mercy admitted.

"Write this down," Marion continued. "On December 16th, I'm hosting a holiday party for the Threes, Twos, and Ones. Each girl is bringing her favorite dish. I'll supply dessert and drinks. Can you come?"

"I wouldn't miss it." Mercy was curious to see how Marion lived.

"Fine. See you Monday, Mercy. And keep your chin up."

"Right. Thanks for calling me."

That evening Mercy put on her leotard and stood before her mirror, expecting to see her neglected muscles sagging. Surprised, she decided she didn't look too bad. Since her injuries had forced her to exist on a liquid diet for ten days, with depression destroying even a wish for food, maybe she'd lost a pound? Time to step on the scale.

To her amazement, she saw the needle drop to her dream mark: a fifteen pound loss! Even if a pound returned when she started eating normally perhaps this ordeal had produced a bright spot. Eileen had said, "No pain, no lose." Neither of them had imagined this kind of pain. But Mercy was glad to put it to some small good use.

Sunday afternoon, Mercy took Dina up on her long-standing invitation to come to her house and use her practice beam.

Mrs. Dibella was leaving with Rose and Theresa as Mercy arrived. Since they'd only spoken on the phone and never met, Mercy was surprised to see that Mrs. Dibella was so petite . . . and so pregnant. Dina had not mentioned that her mother was expecting a baby.

"Hello, Mercy," Mrs. Dibella said. "I'm so glad to

see you're almost recovered! You know we believe you probably saved Dina from getting badly hurt in the accident—we're really grateful to you."

"Oh, sure." Mercy was surprised, since she thought of herself as having caused the accident.

"Go on inside, Dina's in the kitchen," Mrs. Dibella added as she followed her daughters to their car.

Mercy walked through the house, past the den where Mr. Dibella waved while glued to the NFL game on TV, then into the kitchen, where Dina took her coat. "You look so much better this week," Dina said. "The bruises hardly show any more."

Dina took Mercy to the basement exercise mat, where they did stretches. Mercy tried to match Dina's flexibility, but had a long way to go. "This is a fantastic workout room," she told Dina. "No wonder you're improving."

"You can use it any weekend." Dina said. "I mean it."

"Your mom is real sweet. When's she expecting?"

"Umm, April first."

"So you'll have another little sister?"

"My mother says it's a boy. She seems to know, maybe from some test."

"Sure, a brother will be great." Mercy attempted to stretch her spine until her nose touched her instep.

"How is yours doing? Fred, I mean?"

"Much better. My folks and Ernie are down at the hospital now. I just didn't figure they needed me around."

"Will he come home soon?" Dina asked. "I'd like to see him."

"Oh, soon, I guess." Mercy stretched her arms high overhead. "Know what they're all doing? Listening to the Franklin versus Xavier game from the state tournament. It's on the radio. Franklin's probably not going to win without Fred—unless Xavier's star receiver is in even worse shape."

"Guess not." Dina shook out her limbs, walked to the beam, and flipped into a handstand. Talking about Fred's condition made her think of the accident, which gave her chills. Even now she had visions—dreams of darkness and scary sounds—screech, crash, crunch, cries for help, sirens, sobs. But she was getting over it. Mercy, she sensed, was obsessed not with what had happened—but with why.

"What's the news from Flip City?" Mercy asked.

Dina brightened. "All the kids are doing O.K. They can't wait to see you back. Shelley Steiner's in a walking cast. And here's a picture of our new optional uniforms."

Dina handed Mercy a catalogue photo of a leo and jacket.

"If we make optionals, we get these?"

"Not if." Dina wagged her finger. "When. They ordered one for me and Von. We're competing in the first meet in February. Eileen will order for you and the others when you qualify."

"February? Better find out if I can still do a beam trick."

Mercy tried a handstand. She felt slightly dizzy. But

the former thudding pains did not return. She kept trying until she could hold her extension.

"All right!" Dina clapped. "You'll get it back in no time."

Mercy sat on the beam and smiled at Dina, wondering why she felt more at ease in this unfamiliar cool basement than she had felt in her own house for weeks.

Monday night Mr. Dibella drove back from Flip City, where Mercy had returned for her first workout. The girls were still chatting about how much Mercy had accomplished when they pulled up in front of the Samuelses' house. To everyone's surprise, the yard and drive were filled with cars. Kids pushed onto the porch and into the foyer. Mercy guessed instantly. "It's Fred! He's home. That's the Franklin team. Why didn't Dad tell me they were releasing him tonight?"

"Oh, can I just go in and see him for a second? Pop, I just want to see that he's O.K."

"Sure, run in," Mr. Dibella said. "I'll wait."

The girls joined the crowd packed into the Samuelses' living room, but couldn't see over the bodies. "They must have made a bed for Fred in the den," Mercy said. "We'll have to get in line." Players and their dates, cheerleaders and friends, all passed through to greet Fred. No one openly bemoaned the fact that the Franklin team had gotten killed in their tournament game without their star player. Several times the group burst into rounds of the Franklin fight song, followed by roars of laughter.

Mercy was convinced that inside, none of them were laughing; they were angry at the loss of their game.

And the most bitter one must be Fred. She felt like an outsider, thinking, "What if they all know it's my fault? What if every kid at Franklin hates me?"

Eventually she was pushed forward, and Fred spotted her. "Hey, how's it going?" he called to her. "Was this your first workout? Come here, sit by me." Mercy was drawn into the charmed circle of parents, brother, and girlfriend surrounding Fred. He beamed to see her, then waved to Dina who was peeking between two rear guards. "This is my sister Mercy, and her friend Dina. The best jocks I know!" Dina giggled, thrilled to be singled out by Fred's attention. But Mercy's smile was stiff as plaster.

The clock read past midnight as Mercy still tossed in bed, overwrought. Time for the old sleep remedy: a glass of milk and a graham cracker. As she padded down the hall past the bedrooms of her sleeping parents and brother, she remembered that Fred was bedded down in the den. She decided to check on him and be certain he was all right.

The den was lit by the dull silvery light of the TV, flickering as Fred punched the remote control buttons. "Hi," Mercy whispered. "I'm getting milk and crackers. You want some too?"

"No thanks. Too tough to get to the john later."

"Oh. Right." She sat beside him. "What's on?"

"Talk shows. War movie. Hey, look at this." An eerie, wildly scrambled picture flashed across the screen, with a familiar image in the corner. "It's the Playboy Channel. If you're quick, you can catch a few body parts."

Mercy squinted. "You have to be a real pervert to know what you're seeing. Is that a girl?"

Fred lay back and sighed. "Since I'm out of commission, this is all the action I get."

"I know. You're not just missing sports, you're missing . . . everything."

Fred stared at the set, pushing buttons with angry abandon. "Just for a while. God, I wish I could get my hands on the bastard who drove that van."

Mercy felt a lump swell inside her throat.

"I'm so sorry that you and Ernie got hurt. I tried. Maybe if I had swerved to the left instead? I'll always worry . . ."

"No, Fred, Ernie and I are O.K. now. You just have to get well. Then we'll all be super. I'm the one who should be sorry. I mean, I got you into it."

Fred continued to stare at the set, not hearing her. "It's costing Dad a fortune. Car's totaled, my hospital bills, therapy bills, no football scholarship." Fred looked at Mercy. "Maybe Dad won't have enough left for you."

"Me?" Mercy was too upset to follow his thinking.

"I mean, maybe we'll both be out of uniform next season."

Oh. Monthly tuition, meet fees, transportation, that new Optional meet uniform. How much would it all cost? And now that Fred's dreams were dashed, who would care to spend it?

"Don't worry now," Fred said. "You go all the way this year. Get to States, win that trophy. Next year, we'll regroup. Make a comeback."

Fred looked at Mercy with desperate hope. She

nodded, punched off the TV, pulled the quilt over his splinted legs, and went back to bed.

One week after Thanksgiving, Jules's Mother announced she'd bought a condo. "I can't bear to live here through Christmas. It's too much strain on all of us. So I told the management we must move in by December twenty-third. They'll rush the painting and carpeting. Of course, we'll come over here Christmas day for dinner and gifts with your grandparents."

"We're moving so soon?" Jules asked unhappily. "That's just *great*. I'm messing up so badly in English and French that I have to do extra credit work just to pass. And now we have to move? I'll be so distracted that I'll fail everything! Can't I stay home until . . . ?"

"No," Mother interrupted firmly. "I know it's rotten . . . before Christmas . . . when you have problems at school. But I've got to do this. I'll make a new home for us. You'll see."

But when Jules looked into her mother's eyes, she saw about as much fear and uncertainty as must be reflected in her own.

Jules's better moments came at Flip City during her talks with Joe. Each afternoon before workout he devoted a few minutes to hearing her troubles. As Jules told him about her parents' separation, her move from her family home to a condo, her failure to concentrate in school, she forgot her crush on him. She began to think of him as an adviser. She even mentioned being too tall and awkward with the boys in her class. Joe, happily married, confessed he'd once been "too short."

"It all shows up in your problems in the gym," he

said. "When you're out of balance, not eating or sleeping right because you have these worries on your mind, then you lose your balance on the apparatus. If you have no confidence at home, it can take a toll on your gym performance. Try to work on all parts of your life. Let your mother settle things for you at home. Take the tutoring and pull your grades up at school. And you'll see that you'll improve here at the gym."

"But I look so bad now," Jules said. "Flip City is the place where I always felt best. Now I'm losing it here."

"Come on, be positive," Joe urged. "Look at how far you've come. You can see you have more than average talent. So you take it as far as you can, until it stops being satisfying. Then you find some other way to excel. When it's time to leave Flip City, you'll know for sure."

Jules's heart sank at the sad prospect she knew would face her sometime in the next few years. "I hate leaving places. I hate making big decisions."

Joe smiled. "That's growing up. I have to make decisions all the time for the team, and more decisions in my life at home with my wife. We'll be making even more decisions soon."

"What? You're not going away?"

"No. I meant after the baby's born."

Jules's lips formed an O. Marion and Eileen must have known. Were they ever closed-mouthed! Then Jules smiled. Joe, who kept his private life private, had confided in her.

"I guess you don't want me to say a word, so you can surprise us all when she comes."

Joe grinned. "Now how do you know it's a she?"

"Because nobody could be a better father for a girl. You put up with all of us, don't you?"

The following Wednesday after school Jules had no workout. Her book bag was stuffed with extra assignments. On the kitchen table she found a note from Evalene, so she pushed her button on the intercom. "Hi," she said. "You want me to come to your room?"

"Yes, Jewel. We have to talk."

Jules found Evalene sitting on her bed with her old suitcase out on the floor. "Your grandfather said I could take some vacation time. Two weeks. So I'm going to visit my brother and sister in Poland. Been about five years, Jewel."

"You mean after I . . . well, when Mother and I leave?"

"I have airplane ticket for next week."

"But you won't be here when I leave! You won't even be here for Christmas!" Jules was stunned. "You could go any time!"

Evalene looked out the window, where snowflakes drifted through the branches of the oak. "I got family, Jewel. I got to see them. It's better I go now."

Jules realized what Evalene was saying. "You don't want to help me move. You don't want to see it."

"Too hard for me, Jewel. Too hard for us both. This way, your mother will take my place and do for you."

Jules stepped back and swallowed hard. "You're leaving me all *alone*."

"No, I *told* you! It's you and Mother now. Besides, I come back in January, for your birthday, and your state meet."

"Sure. Fine. Don't hurry." Jules bolted from Evalene's quarters, grabbed her book bag, and headed for
the sanctuary of her own room. When dinner was
served she couldn't face any of them. She claimed she
was catching a cold and was permitted to take a tray
up to her bed.

Later she bent over her desk, laboring on an extra-
credit "personal memoir" to boost her low mark in
English. Her choice of topics was "how I feel when
I'm alone." She figured these days she'd be fairly expert on loneliness, since she was losing most of her
family and her old home. She was also faced with
leaving Winchester and Flip City in the near future.

But was "being alone" the same as being lonely?
Jules thought it over more carefully. She remembered
being an only child in a big house, happy in play with
her dolls, or on her backyard equipment, or with one
of the adults. And Evalene always had time to chat
with her or find her small chores, never letting her
feel abandoned. But tonight, it felt different.

She wondered if anybody else ever felt as isolated
in her own home as she did. The adults were occupied
with fighting, negotiating, or avoiding each other. She
didn't ask friends over, for fear they might get caught
in a blowup. Now Evalene was packing.

Jules started a rough draft. "Most of the time, being
alone can be terrible. Certainly it can be terrible when
you want people to be near you and they won't do it.
Then you want to scream. Especially when they say
it's for your own good."

Not a great beginning, Jules thought. She rose,
stretched, did a few spins to loosen up. Then she

thought about gymnastics and how, although you were always part of your team, you were still isolated each time you performed. She'd never thought about her sport before in those terms. So she wrote:

"Being a gymnast, I can see that being alone is not always so bad. Every time you compete in gymnastics, you are singled out. The most special time for a gymnast is when you work alone on the apparatus in front of the judges, with no one to give you courage or share the blame. Some gymnasts think that it is too much pressure. They can't stand being isolated in the spotlight every time they compete. They quit and do other sports where you are always surrounded by your team. But I don't mind that solitary time. I don't see particular faces when I perform. All I see is my apparatus, and my image of myself."

Jules paused. She thought about the new dance steps and tumbling run that the team was starting to learn for the Optionals. She heard the music running through her mind. Although she had not yet mastered the exercise, she remembered feeling graceful and beautiful doing the moves. Jules decided she'd try to put these feelings into the memoir:

"I don't care that I won't ever make Class I or become the star of the gym. I don't even care that I make mistakes and fall on my face. All I care about is that I can get out there on my own and do what I have to do. I feel proud that I'm not afraid to stand by myself. Being alone does not always mean being lonely. That's what we learn at Flip City."

During the rewriting Jules started to get weary. She dropped her head onto her arm and dozed at her desk.

Then she woke to find her mother standing beside her. Mother touched her forehead. "How do you feel?" she asked. "I can see you are working very hard to catch up in your courses."

"I'm a little tired, that's all."

Mother picked up some papers that had slipped to the floor. "What's this? 'It's Fine To Dance Alone.' "

"It's a personal memoir for extra credit. Maybe you could proofread it before I make the final copy?"

"I'd better," Mother said and took the papers.

After Jules performed her evening ritual of cleaning her face, teeth, lenses, and retainer, she stretched out on her bed and read her *USA Gymnastics* magazine. Mother returned, placing the paper on her desk. "I marked a few mistakes. Sentences not complete, punctuation." Then she sat on the bed beside Jules. "I was impressed with the content, though. I can see you are getting a lot more out of Flip City than I ever realized. Doing things on my own has always been important to me, too. But I've had to do so many things over the past years that were important to your father's career that doing things for myself got harder and harder. I always wanted to live up to the Wolcott name. Now, you and I, we're going to have to make our own names."

Jules replied softly: "I guess we can learn to be on our own."

"If you help me, Julia . . . then we can."

Mother kissed Jules's forehead, Clearasil and all, and left.

Jules felt a wave of emotion, realizing Mother could

be hurt also. She could be the one who was truly afraid to dance alone.

Von ate her lunch in the school cafeteria with three Vietnamese boys who had gone to St. Anne's with her. They were sort of self-appointed protectors, and Von usually enjoyed their company. Since they were sophomores, they knew how to get along at Bush. Today, the macaroni wasn't bad and Von was starving, so she let them talk among themselves. After a while she noticed they'd stopped talking and were staring over her head.

"Hi." It was Riccio's voice.

Von spun in her chair. "What are you doing here?"

"Got out of gym class." He leaned over the corner of the table. The three boys didn't budge to make him a space. "This guy got his teeth kicked in during soccer. The teacher panicked and ran him to the hospital. We were supposed to finish the game, but most of us split. I figured I'd find you here."

"Well, you did." Von couldn't think of a clever comment. Her friends were staring suspiciously at Riccio.

"What are your plans for the weekend?" Riccio asked her.

"Umm, let me think." Von smiled up at him, noticing how his cheeks were flushed and his curls blown around from running on the soccer field in the cold. The girls on the bus always said to her, "He's the absolute hottest guy in the sophomore class, and you're so lucky he's interested!" Today he looked handsomer than ever. But she tried to stay calm.

"Same schedule I always have: Gymnastics on Friday night. No meet on Saturday, so I'll work at the café. Homework on Sunday, after family dinner."

Riccio scowled at Von's guardians. "Aren't one of you guys ready to leave?"

"No," they said in unison.

"Come on, Von," Riccio persisted. "Let's find a table, huh?"

"Bell rings in a few minutes," one boy said. "Von, don't cut."

"I won't," Von said as she hurried across the cafeteria with Riccio to an empty table.

"About this weekend." said Riccio. "I thought Sunday afternoon maybe we could take a walk, and talk about French. I need help with conversation. We could *parle*, O.K.?"

"You're a year ahead of me."

"But you're in honors, and I'm slow. We're doing the same stuff. How about it, Von?"

Von had to grin. "So you think we should walk around in the cold and talk French?"

"Right!" he replied. "See, exercise for the mind and body."

"And you think my parents will go for this?" Von laughed. In truth, she was starting to like Riccio a lot more than she should. She found him almost irresistible.

"I bet you could sell your folks on it if you tried."

The bell rang. "I have to run. I'll think about it."

"Saturday when you get your break from the café, come by the bakery. We can talk about Sunday. O.K., Von?"

"Oh, all right." She laughed some more as she dashed to chorus, wondering what she would end up doing about him.

While setting up tables at the café Saturday, Von confided in her sisters about Riccio. "He's the nephew of the people who own the Vasquez Bakery. He's a nice guy, and he wants to take a walk with me and work on French."

Her sisters shook their heads, reminding Von that they were much older than fourteen before Father let them go around with boys. For now her mind had better stay on education.

"Thanks a lot," Von replied sarcastically. "I'm still going to ask Mother. She trusts me. She lets me keep going to gymnastics as long as I make good grades."

"Even Mother won't go for a boyfriend," her older sister said. "Not yet."

Von reported the conversation to Riccio when she ran to the bakery. "My parents don't believe I'm ready to go out."

"I'm not giving up," Riccio said. "I'll get your family to like me sooner or later. Hey, my soccer coach said your brothers were top players at Bush."

"They were, and they do martial arts." Von waved her finger playfully as she left. "So you'd better be good!"

As she skipped back to the café, she felt wonderful inside just from talking to him, almost as high as scoring a 9 on the beam. Although she didn't expect that they'd go out seriously, she still longed to take a walk or two and explore the Romance Language.

As she cleared the Sunday dinner dishes, Von got her mother alone in the kitchen. Diplomatically she described Riccio as a neighborhood friend who wanted to spend time with her, take a stroll and practice their verbs. Loan Nguyen didn't buy the idea. "Don't talk silly! No Portuguese boys speaking French, no walks holding hands in the freezing wind. You are still a young girl, too young for going out with boys, certainly ones from another culture."

"Oh, Mother, please. He's just a friend."

"No, because this could start a bad habit."

"He's not an addiction like cigarettes."

Father had overheard from the hallway, and reprimanded Von. "Do not answer back to your mother! We see many young girls from here start with boys. Many forget their first obligation: to become educated and advance their families."

"Not me, Father. I'm going to college. Nothing will stop me from that goal."

"Fine," said Father. "We are going to see that you don't fall off that path to college, by keeping your mind where it belongs. You will spend this afternoon in your room."

Mother added, "When your sisters were fourteen, they never expected to go out with a boy. Yet all too soon they found young men to marry, and did not finish school. But you and your brothers will graduate. You will have that importance."

"I can do it all. I promise you. But I need some freedom."

Father shook his head. "Is that your dream? Of being 'free'? Let me tell you, little girl, you don't know what that word means. When you are a grown woman, you will see that living for your family is the best way. Everything can be taken from you but your family. That's why you owe them your duty."

"I *know*. That is the Vietnamese way." Von was losing her patience with them. "Up on my desk is my essay and application for the summer school scholarship. You know that if I win, I'll live at the boarding school this summer with lots of kids from different races. And you'll have to trust me. You'll have to let me go!"

"We do not have to do anything," Father said firmly. "We do not have to sign papers for permission."

"Mother?" Von appealed with wide eyes.

"Father and I will see how much work and discipline you show us this year. If you behave, succeed in school and at the gym, and do not run out with boys, we will sign paper for permission. Then if you win this contest, you can go. If you anger us, then we must keep you at home to learn discipline."

Von bit the inside of her cheek to keep from talking back. She did understand that her parents were strict with everyone, even with themselves. They saw plenty of young people in the neighborhood who got into trouble. But why did they take it out on her?

Her parents left her alone to finish the kitchen work. As she scrubbed the sink, she kept seeing Riccio's face in her mind. Just as she was going upstairs to her room, the hall phone rang.

"Hello?" she said quickly.

"Got your walking shoes on, mademoiselle?"

"It's no good. Our outing is out. I have so much

homework, and the final draft of this essay for the competition is due tomorrow. And it's getting late already. . . ."

"What's this competition?" Riccio asked.

"If I win, I get a scholarship for five weeks this summer at a boarding school; it's for minority students."

"What do you want to go away for? If you work at the café this summer, we can see each other every day."

Von paused. She hadn't thought of that aspect before. "I probably won't win," she told him. "And I'll be home most of August anyway. But . . . I want to go, Riccio. I want to live away from home, and learn from meeting new kids. I suppose I'm more ambitious than you think."

"Guess you are," Riccio agreed. "But I'm more stubborn than you think. Because I'm not giving up on seeing you."

Von smiled. "I hope not."

After she hung up, Von went to her room and spread the pages of her essay across her desk. Resolutely, she started to write. The topic was "The Meaning of Minority to Me." In her first draft Von had written about the problem of being part of the Asian minority and holding onto this identity while fitting into the American way of life. But after this week's events, Von decided maybe she wasn't looking deeply enough into the concept. "Being a minority can mean not being part of the dominant group," she wrote. "But it can also mean being different, unique, and special." Von considered how difficult it was not to be one of the crowd in high school, and how important it was to her to stand out in athletics. She found that writing and revising clarified her thoughts. Being Vietnamese made her a minority, but so did the high standards she set for herself, at Flip City as well as in the rest of her life. "I'm not a conformist," Von admitted. "I reach my own goals in my own special way." For she knew that the toughest demands would always be the ones she made on herself.

10

The Party

December 16

"The mailbox says 'Marion Rothman,' " Mr. Dibella announced. "See, we made it in plenty of time, girls. Call me when you want to go home."

"Thanks a lot!" Mercy replied, as she and Dina stepped onto the driveway carrying casseroles. The side door was open. Inside they spotted Eileen, busy setting up Marion's kitchen counters for the dinner. "Hi girls," she called. "Come in! Set your dishes on the stove top. Mmm, smells like meatballs, right, Dina?"

"Uh-huh. Mom's specialty."

"Go across the hall to the living room," Eileen said.

Mercy and Dina discovered a long paneled room with a crackling fire and a picture window looking out on a grove of pines. At the end of the room, a large arch led into an office-den area. Many of the Twos and Ones had already gathered, including Shelley Steiner, who was lounging on the couch.

Mercy smiled. "Hi Shelley. Glad you made it."

"Marion said I had to come. Look, I just have this

lightweight splint. Say, *you're* looking great these days," Shelley said to Mercy.

Mercy made sure that Dina knew all the girls' names. "What happened to Marion?" she asked. "And Joe?"

Shelley replied, "Joe's leading a bunch of parents who weren't sure about following directions, and driving the van full of kids. And Marion's coming back from the bakery with a humongous cake."

Mercy gazed around at the cozy Colonial-style furnishings. "Her house is really warm. I thought it would be businesslike."

"I guess it's like her nest in the boonies," Shelley said. "She likes the quiet life, after Flip City."

"Mercy," Dina asked, her curiosity overcoming her shyness, "do you know what's down in that cabinet?" She pointed to the den, where a glass cupboard lined one wall.

"Those are Marion's awards," Shelley answered. "Americans weren't winning the Olympics in gymnastics when Marion competed. But she's got national medals, certificates, super trophies."

Mercy and Dina knelt in front of the cabinet, where they studied the emblems of Marion's fame. "It's kind of like her biography," Dina whispered.

Mercy rose and looked at the walls of the den. Framed photos covered the walls, photos of Flip City gymnasts from newspapers, shot by parents, or posed by professionals, group shots of winning teams, every winning moment that could be captured on film. Mercy decided these constituted Marion's "family portraits." Then Mercy looked closely at the frame on Marion's desk showing her with her arms around two elderly people. Well, Mercy thought, even Marion must have parents.

"Mercy, when we win States, our team picture will be right here, holding that big trophy." Dina pointed to an empty spot on the wall.

Mercy nudged her. "Hey, we know you're going to win the All-around. You'll get a gold frame!"

Dina grinned, accustomed to Mercy's teasing. "Maybe. I'll bet you could be a great coach like Marion some day."

Mercy was taken by surprise. "Me? I like helping other gymnasts . . . but don't you have to first be a really great athlete to be a great coach?"

"I don't know. If you could, would you love it?"

"Let's face it, Dina," Mercy shrugged sadly. "I'm never going to be a top gymnast. I may never make it to Class II. And my folks may not have the money next year for Flip City."

Dina lowered her eyes. She wanted to think of her teammates all progressing together, going on forever.

A commotion sounded from the kitchen. Several vans had arrived, including Joe's and Marion's, bringing about twenty more girls to the party. Mercy and Dina looked into the kitchen and spotted two familiar brunette heads, one short, one tall. Mercy called, "Hi, Von, hi Jules!"

"Hi guys," Jules said. "Isn't it beautiful out here?"

"Remember when we were in Class IV," Von said, "and we had our team holiday party at Porko's Pizza

Playhouse? That was so wild! But this is much more high class . . . I love it."

As the girls talked, Marion circulated to say hello. Mercy, Dina, Jules, and Von were stunned to see her smartly dressed in a black ribbed turtleneck, dark plaid wool slacks, and silver-and-turquoise earrings, bracelets and pendant, which complemented her silver hair.

"You look so nice out of your sweatsuit!" Von exclaimed.

"Of course," Jules added, "you look nice *in* your sweatsuit."

"And your jewelry is beautiful," Mercy said.

"Thanks, girls. When we went to the Nationals in Albuquerque, Indians sold this wonderful jewelry. I couldn't resist buying it."

"Do you think anybody will make the Nationals this year?" Mercy asked, figuring Shelley's chances were uncertain.

"I surely hope so," Marion smiled. "It's being held in Minneapolis. I may come home with a fur coat for a souvenir!"

As the girls giggled, Eileen walked through the house calling, "Food's ready! Come and line up. Tonight all diets are cancelled!"

Mercy beamed. "Never thought I'd hear that from Eileen."

The girls sat wherever they could find a spot. No class distinctions existed; Ones talked to Threes; nine-year olds laughed with coaches. Only Marion kept moving, busy playing hostess, keeping dishes available and drinks opened. Mercy, Loretta, and Dina were sitting in the corner at the kitchen table. They noticed that Marion finally did fill a small plate for herself with salads, raw vegetables, a hunk of cheese, two meatballs. "Look at Marion," Mercy hissed to Loretta. "She's nibbling like a rabbit, even tonight."

"Yeah," Loretta said, "you'd think she could pig out at the party."

Mercy downed a heavy helping of macaroni casserole and watched Marion with annoyance. "She's probably forgotten what it's like to eat good stuff," she muttered to Loretta.

Dina would rather die than disagree with Mercy. Still, she could not help but observe, "She looks happy with what she has. I bet she just doesn't care about food anymore."

Mercy shook her head. "Unbelievable."

After an hour, Marion announced that cake and coffee was served in the dining-ell. Everyone pressed around the table to smile at the cake bearing the motto in frosting, "FLIP CITY: WHERE THE TEAM IS CALLED THE BEST." As Marion picked up the spatula and prepared to cut, Joe stuck a large lit candle right in the center of the cake. Then he put his arm around Marion, whose head came up to his chest. He held up the other hand for silence.

"Guess you all think this is your holiday cake. Well, as of eight this morning, this cake became the first birthday cake of my first baby, Maryann McCall. Surprise, Marion!"

Marion looked up at him, her hazel eyes sparkling with pleasure. "She's here? Maryann!"

"You all understand that Jane and I named the baby

for Marion. We doubt she will have Marion's great talent. But we sincerely hope she'll have her character."

Applause and cheers rose from the girls and coaches. Joe sent a special wink to Jules, the only pupil who had known his secret.

"Marion," Joe said, "want to blow out the candle?"

Marion managed to do so, but the girls were amazed to see her eyes fill with tears. Joe gave her time to collect herself by whipping out an instant photo of himself in hospital greens cradling a tiny snoozing face next to his own.

"Here's my doll," Joe smiled. "Nurses took it."

Squeals erupted from the girls. Marion examined the picture of her namesake. Masking her emotion with severity, she turned to Joe. "So what are you doing here? You know what I told you months ago. Now that baby is born, I don't want to see you until January. I've hired those two college boys to help the girls work out. We'll miss you, but we'll work twice as hard to keep up the standards. You get back to Jane, who needs you."

"Aw." Joe looked hangdog during this outburst. "You mean I can't even have any cake?"

As the girls giggled, Marion said, "Yes, yes, everyone gets cake. Eileen, hold the plates. How many are we now?"

With the excitement of Joe's announcement, the party got back into high gear. Only Dina clung to the poignancy of the moment, remembering that her mom still had three crucial months before their baby could be delivered. After the cake plates were cleared and some of the girls started dancing to their favorite tapes, Dina still could not shake her reflective mood. She watched the Twos and Ones chat with Marion, respectful but casual. She felt distanced, awed by Marion's reputation. Next year when Dina knew she would be a Two, she hoped Marion would understand her reticence and keep their dealings on a "professional" level. Of course, by next year Dina would have proven herself. She'd have less pressure. And Mom's pregnancy would be over, and her little brother would be just a fact of life.

She wandered over by Mercy's side, listening to Jules and Von encourage her. "You're looking great," Von said, "and you still have a month until States."

"I've dropped a lot of skills," Mercy said.

"But you've qualified," Jules reminded her. "Five of us haven't—including me."

"You'll all make it," Mercy said quickly.

"We're going to Manchester for the Sectional next week," Jules said. "But we won't have Joe. He'll be home with his baby. I guess we'll have Eileen and those new college guys. I hope they're all right."

"Jules, when are you moving to your new place?" Von asked. "My mother will need directions."

"The twenty-third. I'll put my address and phone on some cards and give them out at workout. We're getting the condo redecorated. My room's in lavender and white."

"I bet your mother has great taste," Von said.

"When it's finished, you can all come over," Jules smiled.

"Sure," Mercy said, grinning for Jules's benefit. But

she could hardly imagine how Jules felt, seeing her parents split up and leaving her lifelong home, right before Christmas. "What a bummer," she thought. "I bet she'll miss Joe too, more than any of us."

"Mercy," Dina asked. "Were you surprised about Joe's baby?"

"I sure was!" Mercy said. "And I was pretty surprised when I met your mom, too. You keep secrets better than Joe!"

"Yeah," Dina admitted. "We're having one too."

"Dina, that's so neat!" cried Von.

"Are you glad you're going to be a sister again?" asked Jules. "When is it coming?"

Dina's need to talk overcame her reticence. "It's going to take three more months, but we had two before this one, but they came too soon, and they died, and now Mom can't do too much but rest, because we're all kind of scared." The words tumbled out so fast, she hardly paused for breath.

The girls tried to catch all this over the music and chatter of the party. Finally Mercy asked, "But Dina, you mom's doing O.K., isn't she? She looked good to me."

"She had this cold and flu. I'm not supposed to worry. . . ."

"I know about worrying," Jules said sympathetically. "I worry all the time about Mother and me making it together. But it doesn't change anything."

"Try and think positive," Von told Dina. "You help out at home, do the best you can. And everything will go well."

Jules looked quizzically at Von, who never wasted

energy on fretting or fearfulness. "I wish we could all think like you."

"I shouldn't have talked about it here," Dina said softly.

"Who else can we tell when we have something wrong at home?" Jules said.

Mercy nodded, but kept her own worries private.

By ten the party had wound down; parents and van drivers began to honk to summon their passengers. As Mercy collected her casserole dish, she took one last look at Marion's house and trophy case and photo-laden den. Marion kept a grueling schedule to run Flip City, not only as coach and promoter, but also as businesswoman and accountant. She had no immediate family and little private time. All Mercy could see that she had to give her satisfaction besides Flip City was this pleasant refuge in the woods . . . where she lived a seemingly solitary life. She said to Jules and Von, "I guess Marion never took the time to find a husband. Don't you wonder if she's lonely?"

"Being alone isn't so bad sometimes," Jules answered. "Especially if everybody around you is fighting."

"And besides," Von said, "Marion's the big boss. Like the president of a company. She's doing what *she* wants to do."

Mercy thought that Marion's way of living had its good and bad points. Personally, she didn't think giving all of yourself to your sport and not having a family was for her. As the girls bundled up to leave, Marion stopped the noise and held up her hand. Although she was smaller than half the people in her house, her sense of authority halted the bustle and silenced the crowd.

"I have been thinking this evening," she said, "that some special challenge should be set up for you girls. Although you Twos and Ones do not have your state level meets until spring, you know that the Class III Compulsory State meet is coming up soon in January. This year I believe we have the best Class III team we have ever seen at Flip City. I know you Threes won't see too much of Joe before your state meet, but I'll give you as much of my time as I can. And if we can go all the way together and bring home that team trophy—for which I am installing a new glass shelf in the entrance—I'll give each of you Threes a warmup shirt with your names and 'Class III State Champions' printed on it. I want this state to see that Flip City really can be the best!"

Cheers rocked the air. Even quiet Dina found herself yelling with enthusiasm. Mercy again studied the famed coach and admired the way she could inspire her younger athletes. And Mercy knew that this state meet might be the only chance that she would have to prove herself a winner to Marion. Suddenly she joined in the cheers, realizing she would do anything to achieve that honor.

11

Giving Presents

December 25

Mercy sat on the couch on Christmas morning, awaiting her usual signal. Ever since she was old enough to decipher names on gift tags, her duty had been to distribute the presents. This year she had planned to ask Dad if they could all grab their *own* boxes from under the tree. After all, she was a teenager and had long outgrown the red-flannel-feet pajamas of the Christmas elf.

Now that Fred was crippled and Ernie's wrist was immobilized, Mercy knew there'd be no changing the routine. In fact, she did not want to see her brothers budge from their chairs beside the fireplace. She would play the elf for all it was worth if it distracted the family from her brothers' sorry conditions and made Dad smile—something he seldom did now.

Fred came careening into the room on his crutches, cheerily wishing all a good morning. He was followed by Ernie, his wrist splinted, his lip bearing its usual nick from shaving with his left hand. Mom and Dad came from the kitchen, sipping mugs of coffee. Mercy noticed the usual tray with three hot cocoas waited on the end table—Mom had been up early doing her part.

"Merry Christmas, honey," Dad said, settling into the rocker. "Guess we're ready for the Christmas elf."

As Mercy started hauling out boxes, she thought, "Lucky I'm in great shape, because some of this stuff is heavy." Boxes for Fred included a set of hand weights for his in-house physical therapy program to build upper body strength, plus a portable typewriter to take to college—assuming he went. Mercy felt slightly depressed to see him open these gifts. As it was, Fred exercised incessantly, always doing situps or crawling about on his belly and elbows like a giant slug to stay in condition. Although Mercy understood the doctors had O.Ked all this working out, she still got edgy when he pushed himself to the limit. She sensed a desperation in his activity, which made her guilt over the auto crash even worse. But she kept her elf-like grin glued to her face, and tried to stay in the spirit of the holiday.

From behind the tree, Mercy pulled out two large packages she hadn't noticed before this morning, with her name on them.

"Those are from Ernie and me," Fred announced. "And the other two boxes over there in green, they're to go with them from Mom and Dad."

"It's a group present," Ernie added.

Mercy was touched by all this secret planning on her behalf. "Should I open this long one first?" she asked.

"Sure, hurry up," Fred said eagerly.

Mercy ripped off the papers and discovered a set of downhill skis and poles. The other large carton contained boots, with a pair of woolen ski socks tucked inside of one. "How about those babies?" Fred asked.

"O-o-oh! I can't believe it! They're totally excellent!" Mercy ran her hands over the smooth waxy skis with their shiny bindings. "I've wanted them for years."

"Fred and I argued about whether we should get cross-country or downhill," Ernie said. "I said, cross-country, because once you get to the trails, it's free. No lift tickets."

"But I said, not for Mercy," Fred continued. "She likes to really *move*. She's a real downhill girl."

"And we found out that Schindler has a ski club," Mom said. "You get bus and lift tickets for eight weeks every Wednesday."

"See, that's the day you don't have gym," Dad interjected. "Now look in the other boot."

Mercy removed a hidden envelope and found a certificate and receipt stating she had a membership in the ski club. She said, "George Feder belongs to that club. He loves to ski. He told me that last year they had a fantastic time!"

Fred threw up his hands in a happy shrug. "So this year, he'll have a *better* time! Right?"

Dad winked. "Just keep your eye on the trails and not on the boys." Then he smiled.

"Open the other boxes." Mom urged.

Mercy uncovered a red ski jacket and a pair of ski gloves. She was so delighted she could hardly speak. So she quickly put on the socks, stepped into the boots, then tried on the jacket and gloves. "Well?" she beamed. "Am I terrific or what?"

"Naw," Fred said, "doesn't quite make it."

"You still look like an amateur."

At Mercy's frown, Fred said, "Look in Dad's pocket."

Mercy clumped across the floor in the ski boots to discover a small package extending from her father's robe pocket. When she opened it, she cried, "Wraparounds! Just what I wanted!"

As she slipped on the dark glasses, Fred announced: "*Now* you are *somebody* on the slopes. You're ready to fly."

The presents were perfect. Still, Mercy was torn. She thought: "I'm going to sail on these skis, when Fred has to crawl upstairs. I'm going to navigate with these poles, when Ernie can barely button his shirt. I'm going to the State Compulsory Meet, when those guys will never play football again. Damn, it's wrong, life is so crummy and unfair."

Behind the wraparounds, no one could see the tears sting Mercy's eyes. But her mouth, downturned and wobbly, gave her away. Mom asked, "Did we get something that doesn't fit?"

"Oh. No. I was, uh, just thinking that you probably spent too much on all this, with our bills, I mean."

"But Dad and I planned to get you a new coat and gloves anyway," Mom said. "And the boys got some great bargains."

"Yeah, we got a super deal," Ernie said, hoping to calm his sister before she got weepy, which he hated. "See, the stuff was owned by this girl, but she only used it a few times, and then she turned it in to the

Swap Center. So it's almost new, and just your size, but we paid less than half price for it."

"That's great," Mercy said, trying to steady her voice. "I wonder why any girl would sell beautiful skis like this?"

"Who knows," Ernie shrugged. "Maybe she broke her leg."

"Ern!" Dad shouted. "That wasn't funny."

Ernie sunk his head down into his hand. "Sorry. Damn, I did it again."

"No," Mercy said. "Thanks a million, guys, I mean it. Ern, this time you did it right." But in her heart she knew that Christmas was out of balance this year, and nothing would set it right.

By Christmas night Dina was worn out trying to referee between Rose and Theresa. "I can't stand all this fighting!" she said. "Theresa, if you cry one more time over losing a game, I'm going to make Pop send you to bed!"

"She's a rotten sport," Rose said.

Theresa, exhausted from getting up at dawn, hurled the dice across the room and screamed, "*You* are, Rose!"

Before Dina could come between her little sisters, Mom appeared in the doorway. "Theresa," she said sternly. "Come in the kitchen with me. We're going to have a talk, little lady."

Theresa's lip protruded sadly.

"Over milk and gingerbread boys."

Theresa brightened. Rose's eyes narrowed, envious that Theresa should get a treat for bad behavior.

Mom said, "Rose, why don't you go down in the playroom with Dina? She can teach you the handstand on the beam."

"All right!" Rose grinned at Dina. Permission to work on the practice beam was seldom granted to her. She had plenty of enthusiasm and loved to try the tricks, but she had no natural talent for the beam. Dina winced each time Rose bounded up, tried a simple spin, and flopped off. Even though Rose was fearless, she had no sense of balance . . . just like Anthony . . .

"Sure, let's go, Rose," Dina hustled her sister downstairs before she had any more morbid thoughts.

Dina sat Rose down on the padded mat. "Let's do the stretches I showed you. You have to warm up first."

As they stretched, Rose asked Dina, "Did I hear you tell Mom you're invited to a party on New Year's Eve?"

"Uh-huh, Kelly Ann's. It's a boy-girl party. She's having real punch, and lots of food."

"Wow, that's neat. But why is she having boys? I went to Jean's birthday party last Saturday, and she had boys, and they spilled the soda, so we threw jelly beans at each other."

"Come on, this is a junior high party. Kelly Ann and some of the girls have boys they go out with. So they're invited."

"Do you have a boyfriend?"

"Me? No way." In truth, Dina had been told that two boys who paid a lot of attention to her in English were coming; already she was worried over how to act with them.

"Boys are basically jerks," Rose contended. "I hope you never get a boyfriend and bring him around here."

"Don't worry. I don't even know why I'm going to this party. I'm giving up a twenty-dollar babysitting job. O.K., let's see you try a handstand on the mat."

As Rose flipped over and Dina supported her feet, Dina remembered she'd heard a lot of boyfriend talk at Flip City lately. Von liked a boy in her neighborhood, but her parents forbade her to go out. Von made a big drama out of it, like they were Romeo and Juliet. And Mercy kept mentioning George, whom Dina knew from the halls of Schindler and considered sort of a clown. Dina was scared of the entire interaction she anticipated if she wanted a boyfriend: getting one, avoiding the sex issue with him, eventually losing him. "Rose," she said, "suck in your gut. Feel your back straighten. That's it. Now why can't you do that on the beam?"

Rose landed on her feet. "Because it's *hard*. You fall off plenty of times too, Dina."

"I thought you said I was going to get famous and be on a poster!"

Rose jumped on the beam and tried a spin. "Maybe you will. If you win the state championships, will you get to bring home some big gold medals, like they get in the Olympics?"

"Yes, but I won't win. Too much competition."

"But if you do, Pop's going to buy a set of shelves for your room, so you won't have to fill up your dresser top."

Dina sighed at Rose's big ears and poor spins: the kid overheard every word spoken in the house! Then Dina thought about all those empty shelves awaiting her: Marion had one for the team trophy at Flip City, and now Pop was readying one for her medals to be displayed at home.

"Rose, let me try a few tricks." Dina mounted, but in her weariness on this night after Christmas, she lost her coordination and slipped off during a walkover. She slumped to the mat, thinking that States were only a few weeks away.

Rose said, "Don't worry, Dina. When you have to do it for the team, you will."

"Thanks." Dina gave Rose a half smile. She admitted to herself that she *did* want to win the All-around, because it meant so much to Pop and to Marion and her team, and because she just *did*. But the pressure that went with such a goal brought on the familiar pain in her stomach.

After the main courses of Christmas dinner had been served, Jules excused herself to go up to the bathroom in her old room—and spend a little time by herself. Although she had only moved three days ago with her mother to the condo, she felt as if she had been away much longer. All her old furniture had been left behind since she would be visiting on weekends. But when Jules opened her top dresser drawer, instead of finding her sweats, workout shorts, knee braces, and tube socks, all she found was liner paper and a sachet.

As she went downstairs later for dessert and coffee, Jules peeked into the kitchen. The substitute cook was loading the dishwasher. She smiled briefly at Jules; Jules felt like a stranger in her own home, since Evalene had never been away at Christmas. She was angry at Evalene, but she loved and missed her at the same time. Then she realized that she felt that way about several adults in her world: Daddy, Mother, and even Joe, who had deserted her to stay home with his wife and baby. She knew it was childish to feel this way, but she did.

Everyone had behaved with civilized cool during the dinner, and Jules hoped the truce would continue throughout dessert. As she returned to the table, she was struck with the familiarity of the scene: everyone in their proper places, the sideboard loaded with holiday food. But nothing was really the same. They were all playing parts in a show.

"Now when is that state gymnastics meet?" Daddy asked. "I think it's just *fine* that you made it."

"The fourth Sunday in January," Jules reminded him again. "Remember, you said you wrote it in your datebook." Jules had called him at the bank after she had qualified for States at a meet last week, figuring that at least his secretary would get the information straight.

"Right. I'll certainly try to make it, Julia."

Grandmother added softly, "I am going to attend too."

Everyone stared at her. Jules's father said, "But Mother, the seats are just hard narrow bleachers. And with your arthritis, your back will give out if you sit on them all day."

"I have thought of that, MacArthur," Grandmother replied evenly. "But I won't let it stop me."

"Grandmother," Jules said suddenly. "Remember when I was little and Grandfather went on fishing trips? He had a boat seat. It had a back and sort of a padded seat."

"Imagine you remembering that boat seat, Julia," Grandfather said. "I'd really have to dig around for it."

"I remember a lot of things," Jules said quietly. "Well, Grandmother could put that seat on the bleachers, couldn't she?"

"That's my smart girl," Grandmother smiled. "I'll be there."

Kate shook her head. "Mother, those gym meets can be rather upsetting. There's a lot of noise. And sometimes the girls fall. I mean, there's a great deal of tension."

"I'm not worried about Julia, Kate. If she falls, she will pick herself up again." Grandmother stirred sugar into her coffee. "And we aren't exactly strangers to tension, are we?"

"You can sit with Evalene," Jules told her grandmother. "She's supposed to be back from Poland by then, and even though the meet's on a Sunday, I know she wouldn't miss it."

Jules and Grandmother exchanged smiles. Then Jules glanced hopefully at Mother. For the first time, she realized that part of the reason Mother avoided meets was that she was frightened of the risk involved and didn't like the stress and shouting. Mother was really a very reserved person. Maybe she had not always been the social smash that she appeared to be?

Kate Wolcott spoke to her mother-in-law. "You can sit by me, Mother. I wouldn't miss it either."

Jules didn't know what to say. She was proud of the unaccustomed attention she was receiving—but she also worried that she might blow the meet, with so many people watching her.

That night Jules and her mother relaxed in the quiet of their snug living room, which still smelled of fresh paint and starched fabric. Mother sipped a small sherry, then gazed at Jules over the glass. "I was proud of you today. You did beautifully over there. It was almost like being up on that balance beam."

Jules blushed. "I guess it was." She looked around the condo, wondering if she'd ever get used to living there. Then she thought out loud. "Next year at this time I'll be 'visiting' from school, won't I? I'll be a visitor here and a visitor there. Weird."

Mother paused thoughtfully. "Maybe not," she said.

"You mean next year maybe I won't go to boarding school?"

"I said, maybe not." Mother looked at the gateleg table in front of the double window. "Next year we should put our own small tree up there."

Jules couldn't help pushing the issue. "But maybe next year at this time, you and Daddy will be back together?"

Mother looked kindly at Jules. "Maybe not," she said.

*   *   *

Although the Nguyens' favorite holiday was the Vietnamese New Year, which fell in January this year, Von still had a special fondness for one symbol of American Christmas: the tree. In school she had asked Riccio if he and his mother decorated a tree in their apartment. He said they were going to trim the tree at his uncle's house. When he talked about the lights, ornaments, tinsel, and angels, Von's eyes sparkled. "I wish I could see it," she murmured.

"Come on, Von, won't your father let you come over to my uncle's for a visit? That's no big deal, is it?"

"They're all determined not to let us do things together. Maybe when I'm older next Christmas, they'll let me come."

Riccio frowned. "You aren't waiting until then." And he marched off with no explanation.

On Christmas night, a loud knocking sounded at the Nguyen apartment. The family had served a noon dinner at the café and were now relaxing in the living room over tea. Mr. Nguyen opened the door and was surprised to find a tall boy holding a small bush. "Yes?" he said.

"Hello, Mr. Nguyen, I'm Riccio Vasquez, and I have a present for Von."

Although Mr. Nguyen realized this must be the Portuguese fellow who was pursuing his little girl, courtesy required that he admit him. Von rushed to the door as she heard Riccio's voice. Then she saw his amazing gift.

"Oh Riccio, it's a Christmas tree!"

"Boy, was it tough riding it over on my bike! Excuse

me, Mr. Nguyen, but can I set this on the table and plug it in, so I can show Von how it works?"

"Works?" Father frowned deeply. Von's mother and sisters gathered to see the curious present. "Yes, well, put here." Father pointed to a lamp table beside the couch.

The miniature tree, made of artificial green brush-branches and trimmed with bright strings of glass beads and tiny balls, was set into a metal musical stand. As Riccio plugged in the cord, strands of little white lights twinkled, and the tree turned slowly while a music box played "Silent Night." Von and her sisters clapped and laughed softly. Even her brothers stooped beside the table, delighted with the tree.

Von saw that the tree was expensive and hard to find. She'd never seen anything so lovely in local stores. "You went to a lot of trouble," she said. "Thank you so much."

"Sure, it's nothing," Riccio grinned, sticking his chilled hands in his pockets.

"Mother, look, he rode his bicycle in the cold. We must give him a cup of tea, don't you think?"

Although Loan Nguyen also thought the gift was lovely, she could spot a boy who knew how to win a girl's heart. Still, he was just a boy with a chill, wasn't he?

"Come," she said. "Sit in here." She led the two of them into the kitchen and poured cups of steaming jasmine tea. Then she stood back. "You never catch cold if you drink this tea," she told Riccio. "So. You like to watch Patriots?"

"The Patriots?" he asked in surprise. "Oh, sure."

"Me too. Bad this year, huh?"

"Bad defense," Riccio agreed, thinking it odd to talk football with Von's mother. "Need more muscle."

"Look for bigger boys," Mrs. Nguyen nodded. "Next year maybe."

"Right. I play soccer myself."

"Ah, soccer. My sons too."

"We didn't do well this year at Bushnell. Guess we needed some guys like your son Hai."

Mrs. Nguyen smiled, knowing the family would not stand a chance against this determined fellow's charm. "Von, pour more tea." She backed out gracefully, leaving Von in charge.

"Better drink slowly," Von said with a grin. "When the tea is gone, so are you."

"Come on, your mom is crazy about me."

"Not yet," Von said more seriously. "But they love the tree. So do I."

"It's a start," Riccio said.

Von folded her hands on the table beside her teacup. Riccio put one of his larger ones over them. Von whispered, "Every night I'm going to turn off all the lights and watch the tree shine in the dark. It'll be like magic."

"Von," he asked. "Did you enter that contest for that summer school scholarship?"

"Yes. We're supposed to hear sometime in January."

"You really like to win, don't you?"

She nodded. "I like to learn too. Partly it's because my family encourages me so much. They're all behind me. And partly it's just me. I know I won't ever be the most superior student or the greatest gymnast in the world. But I don't want to be just average and let life pass me by."

Riccio grinned. "You could never be average."

"Doesn't your family have a dream for you?" she asked.

"My mother wants me to make a good career for myself, mostly because I'm the only son. But I don't think she cares what it is."

"You'll do fine," Von said. "I'd buy anything you had to sell. In fact, I do, every time I go to the bakery!"

"Thanks," he said. "Maybe some of your winning streak will rub off on me."

"My winning streak may end on January twenty-second," Von said. "That's the State Compulsories for Class III, over at Franklin High."

"I'll be there, yelling for you," Riccio assured her.

"Then I've got it made." She smiled.

"Von . . . is your father staring at me from behind?"

Von raised her love-struck gaze. "Uh, yes. Tea's over."

Riccio rose, winked at Von, then turned and extended his hand, "Merry Christmas, Mr. Nguyen," he said.

Von's father hesitated. Then he shook Riccio's hand.

12

Secrets

January 20

After what seemed like an hour of slow driving, silence broken only by the whack of the wipers and the splash of sleet, Mercy and Dina were delivered to Flip City by the Samuels boys. Ernie, whose wrist had almost healed, drove; Fred kept him company. Before she even left the car, Mercy's nerves started to get tight. By the time she was in the locker room, she was already dreading this final workout before the state meet. Once she had thought it would be an exciting challenge to be coached by Marion. But now, after a month of being ridden hard by the Boss Lady, Mercy was not so thrilled. Marion had been dividing her time between vault and floor, her favorite events, letting Eileen remain beam coach and having the new man, Mike, take over on bars. While Marion was not so severe on the vault, she had been picking the floor exercise apart bit by bit, until Mercy thought she'd scream. Eileen had been demanding, but Marion was brutal.

Mercy and Dina joined Von, Jules, and the other Threes sprawled on the spring floor, as Marion paced deliberately along the side. Eileen and Mike stretched out on some mats, sipping Mountain Dew, preparing for a six-hour stretch of intense coaching.

Jules asked the others, "You all done with final exams?"

"Yeah. Thank God." Mercy sighed. "Ernie coached me all week in math. The rest I was up for. How about you?"

Jules nodded. "We won't get the grades until Monday. But I think I got at least a C in everything. I'd better. My life depends on it."

"I have a lot riding on my grades too," Von said. "Most of the exams were easy, except for science. I can't tell those dumb rocks apart, even though my brother Hai kept quizzing me."

Dina flexed, then extended her feet as far as they'd go, keeping her eyes lowered. She knew it was silly, but listening to them talk about their big brothers made her feel sad.

"How about you?" Jules asked Dina. "I remember my first exams in seventh. Nasty!"

Dina nodded. "I'm so glad they're over. So we won't have anything on our minds during States."

As the older girls spread out in a circle, several of the younger Threes leap-frogged over the beams, hopped on mats, jumped into handstands and then sprang into the air. Marion walked onto the floor and spoke in her low penetrating voice. "The only girl doing any serious stretching is Dina. The rest of you get busy. Now."

Dina blushed to be singled out, even for praise. She

saw Mercy send her a disgruntled look as she pushed her torso down over her extended leg. Mercy then whispered to the girls, "Marion's going to kill us tonight. I can see it. Doesn't she know how tired we are from taking finals?"

As she grumbled, Mercy could remember Joe's regular speech on that subject: a good gymnast gets her academics done first, she works ahead on weekends, uses free Wednesdays and study halls, reviews for tests at home after workout. Joe claimed a girl could manage it all if she cared enough about both and got her priorities straight. Mercy surely missed Joe tonight.

After stretches, Marion assembled the girls around her for a talk. The young ones were still edgy, doing seat-spins on the mat. Marion raised her hand. The youngsters quieted.

"You can see that we have ten Threes qualified for States: five of you in the nine-to-eleven group; and now that Loretta has turned twelve, we have five in the twelve-to-fourteen group. You may know that the bigger gyms will have fifteen or twenty, and we'll have ten on our team. This doesn't mean we can't win. A top-five score in each event can do it. It means that every score from Flip City will count. Even your weakest event will be important."

As Marion's hazel eyes focused on the upturned faces, Mercy thought instantly about her bars routine. Any of them could have a bad meet, slip on the floor, lose their balance on the beam, or flop their landing after a vault. But Mercy knew she was a consistent drag to the team on bars. She stood a chance of blowing the team's average with a really poor score. Mercy believed they all knew it; her ears began to burn.

Marion continued: "I know you've felt Joe's absence. He'll be there Sunday to coach you on vault and bars. But what you do here with Eileen, Mike, and me can make a difference, give you the edge. That's why I want each one of you to go the full distance tonight. Now let's work."

Mercy stared up at Marion, mesmerized. Eileen never talked quite like that, so seriously and powerfully. Why did Marion expect that one night's workout could alter a girl's self-image and affect her performance? What could one night do for you?

"We have almost three hours," Marion concluded. "I'll send each of you where you need it most. Starting with Mercy." Marion spun on her heel and studied Mercy as if she was a large lump of moldable clay. "Your vault is back on top, so just run it a few times. Then get to the bars with Mike. I want to see a solid hour of work on your routine. Then to the beam with Eileen, and finish with me on the floor."

As Marion moved on to Jules and Von, Mercy doubted that she would improve much from an hour with Mike. He was too inexperienced to notice how her exercise had deteriorated—or to whip her into shape fast. Well, Marion would be so busy criticizing floor exercises that she'd hardly notice. . . . Then Mercy faced the fact that something was wrong with her attitude. Although she was worn out after a week of school pressure and agitated from so many previous workouts with Marion on her case, she knew she should still be eager to accomplish a lot tonight.

Instead she was trying to hide from her coaches and herself. Why, she wondered, was her mind so messed up?

As she jogged over to the bars and started a few warmup swings, Mercy decided that part of her problem was that her nerves were so ragged at home. Although he no longer played ball, all the family talked about was Fred. When his splints came off soon, would he walk? Run? Climb? Would the grueling therapy program he was starting make him like new? Mercy felt that they were all waiting for Fred to be "born again." As usual, nobody paid much attention to her. Dad wasn't even coming to States. He had a chance to work overtime and said they needed the money.

"Hey Mercy," Mike called to her. "Get going with your routine. Marion's going to come over later and check on you."

"Oh, terrific," Mercy said. "Is she really?"

"Yep, so start swinging."

Mercy chalked her hands, then pulled on a pair of palm grips she'd used since Christmas to protect the callouses on her hands. The grips sometimes slid and loosened her tight hold on the bars; but they saved her from getting rips. She planted her feet, then glanced at the clock: forty-five minutes to correct all the flaws in her exercise and impress Marion. Sure. Nothing to it.

Soon Loretta and Amy arrived to take turns on the bars, since it was also their weak event. Accustomed to getting a grin, a joke, some friendly encouragement from Mercy, the younger girls stood aside and waited for her. But Mercy had no good humor for anyone. Muttering curses at her own ineptitude, she pushed through her routine. The moves were solid now, the kips were strong, but she still had many stops and faults. Eventually Mercy's exercise actually did improve. By the end of the hour, when Marion watched her work, Mercy got a sober nod. "O.K., hold this level for Sunday. It's all in your concentration now."

"Uh-huh." Mercy edged away from the bars. "Should I go over to Eileen?"

Marion gave a small grin. "Can't wait to get on the beam? That's what I like to see."

"Well, only when it follows the bars," Mercy admitted.

Marion shrugged. "At least you're honest."

Working beam with Eileen, however, proved to be as demanding. Mercy slipped and wobbled, blowing her timing on each pass. Often Eileen stopped her to reposition hands and feet, align hips, telling her, "*feel* that line from your head down to the beam! And clean up those poses, every finger in place." At last, Eileen pronounced Mercy's routine up to par. "You got it back. See you in the weight room after you do your floor with Marion."

Mercy's head snapped around to face Eileen. "Weigh-in? Come on, Eileen, not tonight! Give me a break!"

"It's Friday night," Eileen said simply. "Anyway, you don't look like you're up, so what's the fuss?"

"Who cares if it's Friday," Mercy interrupted, a ragged crack starting in her emotional shell. "I just can't handle it. Not now, before States. . . ."

Eileen looked stunned. "Mercy, what's this garbage? We don't discuss weighing in. You have to qualify to compete."

"There's only *five* of us," Mercy shouted. "You know damn well Marion won't kick me off the team over a lousy pound!"

Eileen's small hand barely encircled Mercy's developed bicep, but she shook her hard. "Stop that stuff! You know Marion would forfeit a chance to win States rather than let a girl compete who was over limits! This is a professional gym, and you're a professional gymnast. Now start acting like one!"

Mercy felt that hot wave of emotion rise up and sting her eyes. "O.K., right." She swallowed. "Sorry. I need a drink."

Eileen exhaled and gave Mercy's shoulder a pat. "Sure. I don't know how we ended up yelling at each other. Go on."

Mercy dashed for the drinking fountain.

As she bent over and gulped large cool swallows, she saw Dina appear at her side. She splashed a little water on her face. Then she tried to look composed.

"Are you O.K.?" Dina asked. "You look pretty wrung out."

Mercy noticed that Dina was damp with sweat, her leo glued to her flat little stomach. "I'm O.K. You do floor with Marion?"

"Yes. She killed us, like you said."

"So, did you hear me? I mean, yelling at Eileen?"

Dina frowned. "We heard something. . . . Not much."

Mercy glanced at Marion, who was busy criticizing Von. She knew she'd better face the Boss Lady and get through it.

When she reported to Marion, she was told, "Let's see what you've got left in you." Marion sat on a pile of mats beside the floor. "Mercy, I want to see you use your strong points. Run harder, pump those legs, get good height. Jules, cue the tape!"

Mercy struck her starting pose. Marion called to her: "Chin up. Head back. Shoulders straight. Give me performance!"

So Mercy gave what she thought was "performance." Without budging from her position on the mats, Marion sent a running stream of criticism:

"Watch your position. Straight lines on the floor. That's it. Now stretch that extension. No, punch the floor. Harder! Feel the height in those straddle jumps. Never look down! Feel when you aren't on the money. There, that's a tenth deduction! O.K., be sharp, give me precision steps . . . tight legs. Point those feet. Give me *more*."

Never could Mercy recall working harder. She finished off balance but on the beat. Her heart banged her ribs, her lungs ached, her chest heaved as she sucked in air. Von, Jules, and Loretta stood by the tape player and watched, for Marion made each girl pay close attention to her teammates' exercises. No gossiping or lolling around, she said. Learn from others' mistakes. A pro listens to all critiques, said Myth Marion.

Marion stared at Mercy. "The only word is half-assed. I know you can do a superior routine. I've seen you. Let's hope the old theater saying is true: bad dress rehearsal, good show. Because you're going to need it."

Still trying to catch her breath, Mercy doubted she'd find the strength to give even more.

"All right, Jules," Marion continued. "One more time for you. Let me see it all, beautiful line, from your arm position down to your toes. Sharp perfect steps. You can do it!"

Jules tossed back her hair, which lay in damp strands on her forehead. Her eyes widened with new hope that she could show Marion how much she'd learned. As the music blasted, Jules pushed herself to the outer limits, and did show real performance, more strength and confidence. Although she missed Joe, she knew she'd improved with Marion, whose demanding techniques had worked for her.

Mercy also noticed Jules's improvement. Before she could figure out why her own routines were so erratic, she was up again. As she ran the routine one more time, she could hear along with the pounding beat of the music the steady chant from Marion: "Give me more, more, more . . ." Mercy knew that a girl of her age and experience should be showing more power, precision, grace, maturity, all qualities that were needed in a compulsory floor exercise. Instead, she felt less coming from her, as if the plug had been pulled on her emotionally. As she completed the routine, she waited for the barrage of criticism from Marion.

"O.K. That was better."

Better? Mercy was so exhausted, she hardly cared.

"Now next time . . ." Marion continued. Then she stopped. Two young men entered the far door and stood against the wall. Mercy glanced over and recognized the snow-dusted jackets of Fred and Ernie. Dina also saw them, and dashed over from the vault runway to find out why her father had not come to pick them up.

"Your dad called us," Ernie explained. "He's stuck in New London with a dead battery. With the bad weather, he won't make it home until tomorrow. So we volunteered to run you guys home."

"Oh, thanks." Dina smiled with relief. "I thought for a minute maybe he had some problem, like with my mother, or, well, O.K., we'll be finished soon."

"We'll hang out here," Fred said. "I'm not crutching it up to that gallery." He waved at Mercy, then tried to make his way around some equipment to seat himself on the stack of mats where Eileen had rested earlier. But his crutch caught under a springboard, and Fred went flying face forward onto the floor.

As the thud of Fred's body sent vibrations through the springs, Marion jumped up and ran over to him.

"Are you O.K.?" she asked.

"Sure, sure," Fred said, raised on his elbow. "I fall a lot. This time I almost bounced."

Marion smiled, then backed off and let Ernie hoist his brother over to the mats. She could see that the boy had only had the air knocked out of him; the buoyancy of the spring floor had kept him from getting hurt. But when she walked back to her place on the far side mats, she did not find Mercy.

She called to Jules and Von, "Where is she?"

"Bathroom, I think." Von offered. In truth, neither of them had seen Mercy bolt for the door and vanish. Their eyes had all been on Fred.

Mercy, however, had not run to the bathroom, a place where sounds could be heard by any girl going to the weight room or the drinking fountain. She'd raced up the stairs to the viewers' gallery, empty of parents on such a miserable evening, then disappeared into Marion's office, the Penthouse.

Although she tripped over boxes of files and stubbed her toe, Mercy found a dark corner to sit in, beside Marion's desk. With knees drawn up tightly she huddled and wrapped her arms around herself, trying to keep her control from shattering completely. Then for the first time in her life at Flip City, Mercy totally lost her discipline. She had to cry it out.

Dina, the only one who saw Mercy's escape and guessed where she went, took another turn at vaulting. She watched the clock, deciding to give Mercy a while to get herself together. But she felt uneasy. Something was really wrong with Mercy. Since the coaches were paying little attention to her at that moment, Dina darted out of the gym.

In the gallery she heard the low soft sobs coming from the Penthouse. She crept inside and stooped by her friend.

"Don't cry about Fred. He's O.K."

Mercy tried to gesture, then speak; but her voice failed.

Dina handed her a tissue from a box she found on the desk. "Fred's going to get well. I know it."

Mercy blew and sniffed. "I guess. Tonight, it was all too much. I cracked up. Can't stand . . . to watch him."

"Come on, he's doing better."

"Maybe his legs are ruined." Mercy whispered the words she'd never said aloud. "It's my fault. I made him go that night, made him stay too late. I did it. . . ."

"No!" Dina snapped. "I was there. We had an accident."

"Yes, but Dina . . ."

"Never take the blame for an accident!" Dina spoke with unusual force.

"But Fred's life won't ever be the same."

Dina took a deep breath. "Maybe it won't. But my brother's life is over."

Mercy looked at Dina's face, barely outlined in the dim light. "Your brother?" she echoed.

"I never told anybody down here about Anthony. But I'm going to tell you. Because you and I have the same thing wrong with us."

Dina didn't want to watch Mercy's expression while she talked, so she gazed out the windows over Marion's desk.

"He was three years older than me. We were best buddies. He was a perfect athlete, so good at baseball that the high school coaches came to see him play

Little League, saying he'd play varsity his freshman year. He was a daredevil too. He'd try anything. So that spring, we had an early thaw, and Anthony was itching to get out into the country on his bike. He dared me to follow. He always dared me to do stuff that was against the rules. We rode way out of our neighborhood, down a highway, and we came to these reservoir grounds which were behind a locked fence. But Anthony dared me to climb over the fence. Then we hiked around the grounds. Anthony kept talking about the baseball season starting. I was excited just to be out with him. Then we came to the reservoir wall, with signs telling everyone to keep off. We loved to play trapeze and high-wire, so we always walked any wall we found. This time I was scared. The wall was too high, and I was afraid someone would see us trespassing. Anthony pulled himself up and he started to walk the wall. I guess he looked down at me. Because I was crying. And he lost his balance and he fell. Into the reservoir."

Dina heard the familiar tinkling of the floor music below, but it came from miles away. And she heard echoes of her cries.

Mercy's face was rigid. "Dina," she whispered. "How terrible for you. Don't tell me any more."

"You have to listen now," Dina continued. "I jumped up and I lay on top of the wall and could see into the water. But he wasn't treading—he was gone. I screamed his name forever. Some workman found me hanging over the wall and carried me away. It was a long time before they found him."

"No Dina, this is so bad. . . ." Mercy wanted to cry for Dina, but she was wept dry of tears. "How did you live through it?"

"I don't know. I never talked to anybody about it. But see, Mercy, it was an accident. So I work hard at the gym, and look out for my sisters, and pray my mom will have another boy. My sisters don't remember Anthony too well now, so they don't know how . . . well, they don't hate me."

Then Mercy made a connection. "Dina, don't you really talk to your folks about how it was when you climbed on that wall?"

"They don't like to talk about Anthony. It's too hard."

"No, Dina, I mean talk about you. How much you miss him. How you still feel. I mean, at least your parents can see why it's so hard for you to get up on the beam. You must talk about that?"

"What do you mean?"

"I mean why you've got such a fear of falling. The beam must remind you of the wall."

Although Dina felt rather numb, she sensed tears brimming in her eyes. "I never thought about it like that."

"Oh God, Dina."

The girls sat in silence for a few minutes. Finally Mercy was compelled to offer some advice. "I think you should say something to your folks."

Dina brushed away the tears. "I don't know how."

"I know it's tough to think of what to say. It isn't just going to come up at the dinner table. But if you're only doing gymnastics to make up for what you think they're missing without your brother, then that's no good. If you're punishing yourself or something, that's no good. You can talk to your folks, Dina. You have to."

"It's hard enough to talk to you about it," Dina admitted.

"You did it, though." Mercy managed a smile.

"Do you talk to your folks a lot about Fred?" Dina said. "About how bad you feel?"

"Fred?" Mercy was taken aback. "What's to say? I mean, they're so worried about him all the time. . . . They don't want to hear from me. It doesn't matter. . . ."

"But Mercy, when Fred fell down tonight, you had to run up here and cry."

"That was a lot of stuff piled up. Let's forget it."

Dina didn't know what else to say. She'd given Mercy all she had to give. She'd promised to try and take Mercy's advice. But Mercy wasn't taking Mercy's advice. Dina rose. "We better go down. It must look really weird that we're gone so long."

Mercy and Dina did not speak again during the nerve-wracking ride home. They huddled down in the back seat, belts tightly cinched, and prayed that the sleet would not grow worse. Ernie navigated the roads with extreme caution. As they pulled up in front of the Dibella house, Dina, exhausted from a day of exams, workouts, and dark revelations, had dozed off. Mercy gave her a nudge.

"Sorry," Mercy whispered, "about being bitchy tonight."

"That doesn't matter," Dina replied. "I'll try and do what you said . . . if you'll do it too."

Mercy nodded but made no reply. "See you Sunday."

At home, Mercy and Ernie helped Fred up the sleet-covered driveway into the front foyer. As they made it into the house, they heard their father on the hall phone.

"Dad, they just made it home," he was saying. "Mercy," he turned, "it's Grandpa. They're going to set out tomorrow morning and wanted to know what we thought about the weather conditions."

"Let me talk to him," Ernie offered, and took the receiver. "Hello, Grandpa? It's Ernie. Yeah, I just drove home from the gym, and we have a little sleet here. But they say it's going to stop tomorrow, and I guess the highways will be clear. Right. . . ."

Mercy dropped her gym bag with a thud and shouted, "Ernie, the roads are terrible! Don't let them come!"

As she stood beneath the foyer light fixture, the harsh beam revealed a face both lined with fatigue and puffy from weeping. Her cheeks were stained by rivulets of sweat and tears. Mercy's father looked at her with a frown. Her mother came over to her from the living room. Even Fred, resting on the steps, rose to stare at her.

"Hold on, Grandpa," Ernie said, then clapped his hand over the mouthpiece of the receiver. "I was doing the driving," he reminded Mercy, "and it wasn't that bad. And Grandpa's truck can hold the road. Don't you want them to come for . . ."

"For *my* meet? And what if something happens?" Mercy couldn't begin to verbalize the visions of her grandparents in an accident; frightening flashes of their smashed truck crossed her mind. "I don't want any part of this!" she yelled at all of them. "Just do what you want!"

Mercy shoved past Fred and bolted for her room.

Later, while curled up in her favorite pair of Ernie's outgrown thermal underwear, Mercy heard a knock on her door. Although she mainly wanted to hide, she had to admit her mother.

"Mercy, your dinner is in the oven."

"O.K. I'll be down in a while."

"Grandpa is going to check in the morning with the state police. If road conditions are better, they'll drive over."

"Doesn't matter if they come," Mercy said. "I'm not going to win. It's not worth Grandpa taking any chances."

"Grandpa has been taking his chances for sixty-eight years, honey. And he doesn't care if you win. You're his sunshine. He just wants to see you perform. Especially since maybe it's your last year."

Mercy sat up. "You mean because I won't win?"

"I don't know about winning," Mom said as she sat on the edge of the bed. "I meant not knowing how things are going to work out. With our finances and Fred's college expenses and all, it's hard to say what we can manage next year."

Mercy nodded. Fred had warned her about this problem.

"See," Mom continued, "we can't predict how

everything will happen in this life. Maybe Dad and I will get raises. But maybe we'll get laid off. Who knows? A lot of things happen that are out of our control, honey. We can't blame each other."

"Yes," Mercy blurted out, "but what if it's really our fault?"

"Mercy, you're acting strange tonight," Mom said. "Did you have a fight with your coaches?"

"No. I sort of yelled at Eileen, but she got over it."

"Trouble with your weigh-in?"

"No, I was on the mark."

"Nervous about the state meet?"

"Not now. Probably I will be . . . it's just hard for me to talk about it."

"Mercy . . . I don't know if I should tell you . . . but while you were driving home tonight, I got a call from Marion Rothman."

Mercy was startled. "What did she tell you?"

"Oh, nothing bad. She said she'd been riding you girls pretty hard this month, but she figured you all could take it. She knew *something* was bothering you though. Tonight, she decided, maybe it was about Fred."

Mercy pursed her lips, angry that Marion had stuck her nose into Mercy's private fears and guilts. Now what could she say to Mom?

Mercy's mother continued. "Marion said she never saw you in a fix you couldn't handle before. So I thought, what's Marion see that I don't? Mercy doesn't have problems. She the *good* one! Ernie's got some problems, and Dad and I, we know that. And sure, Fred's got his problems too. But somehow you just kind of slipped right under our noses, honey. Is Marion right? What's tearing you up?"

"It's Fred!" Mercy felt the tears threaten again. "Mom, Dina figured out how I feel and she told me this terrible secret true story. She had an older brother, and they dared each other to do things, and she distracted him once and he fell and got killed. Mom, it was an accident. Like ours was. But she still blamed herself. And because of how she felt, she figured out I was blaming myself too. For our accident. So she got up the nerve to tell me."

Mother fingered the quilt on Mercy's bed, a lovely patchwork that had been her mother's and hers, and now was her daughter's. "I can't explain why things happen. We all have to come to our own truth. But never blame yourself for what happened that night after Thanksgiving. It just happened, and we're all going to get over it."

"I guess you're right," Mercy said, still struggling to cough up the rest of her guilt. "But it was my meet and my friends. So it'll still be my fault until the day I die."

Alma Samuels rolled her eyes toward the ceiling. "Ernie says, 'Mom, it was my turn to drive, so if I'd been driving it wouldn't have happened to Fred.' Then Fred says, 'If I'd swerved the car the other way, it wouldn't have happened at all.' How about if I never got married? Then I wouldn't have any of you to bug me and *nothing* would have happened!"

Mercy sighed. "O.K., I see your point. But I'll always know that if it hadn't been for me, Fred would still be perfect."

Her mother gave an incredulous grin. "Fred's not perfect!"

Mercy blurted out, "He is! At least you and Dad think so!"

"Come on, Mercy. Maybe Dad doesn't always like to face it, but Fred isn't any great brain. Not in stuff like math and computers and business. And he's too easy to be a great salesman. I worry a lot about how he's going to make a good living."

"You do?" Mercy was amazed. "But Fred's so sweet . . . and you and Dad think he's . . . well, I always thought . . ."

"Sometimes I don't know *what* you think," Mom replied. "Oh, I guess it seems like we pay more attention to Fred, with football season and his making college plans. But we sure don't think he's perfect. You and Ernie and Fred are all the same to us, honey— *ours.*"

Mercy nodded, still digesting the news that Fred Samuels was just an ordinary mortal like herself.

"Next time you have a problem or think you're getting the short end around here, tell me. Don't make me hear it from Marion."

"I won't." Mercy sighed. "So how about that casserole? Is it baked into cement?"

"When's the last time I served you a cement casserole?"

"Well, last month . . ." Mom gave her a poke. "Just kidding."

After Mom left, Mercy rummaged through her hamper for a semi-clean sweatshirt, knowing she hadn't done her laundry in so long that her dresser was nearly empty. Her room had needed cleaning for weeks. And when was the last time she'd gone out with her friends? Her priorities, like her room, had gotten disorganized.

But Flip City, Mercy knew, took so *damn* much time. No wonder she never found time to tell Mom what she thought. That Marion . . . too bad, Mercy thought, that I'll never make it to Class II and work with her. She's some kind of mind reader to have figured me out. But she did call Mom and get us talking . . . and that felt good.

13

Compulsory States

January 22

At noon on Sunday Mercy and Dina arrived to find Jules and Von in the crowded lobby of the Franklin High athletic building. Mercy called to them, "Hi, guys! Have you heard how the kids made out this morning?"

Jules responded, "We just got here too. Let's go find Eileen in the locker room."

The girls knew that their younger teammates had their Class III competition that morning and hoped devoutly that their friends had scored high in their division. The four forged ahead into the locker room filled with gymnasts from the twelve to fourteen age group, representing a dozen schools throughout the state. Seated on a corner bench with feet propped, Eileen took a needed rest, since she'd been working all day.

"Hi Eileen," Mercy called. "How'd the kids make out?"

"Super!" Eileen replied. "Everyone got a medal for placing in at least one event. Not bad, considering we had one of the smallest teams. Now you girls are going to have to hustle to bring up our overall team average."

"I remember that first-place team trophy from last year," Von said. "It looked like a huge gold skyscraper with wings. That's the one *we're* going to win."

"The younger girls aren't at the top, but their scores overall are good enough that if you really hit it your combined scores can pull if off," Eileen assured them.

Loretta, their fifth group member, dashed up with more news. "Guys, guess who's out there ready to cheer for us? Joe's baby!"

"Come on, you're kidding!" Mercy said. "Where?"

"Joe's wife has her in one of those baby baskets over in the seats behind the vault runway."

"I can't wait to see her," Jules beamed. "Is she the cutest little thing? Does she look like Joe?"

"Without the moustache," Eileen laughed.

"Is Marion here?" Mercy asked, already nervous about seeing her.

"She's coming," Eileen replied. "Now get dressed. Warmups start soon."

As Mercy, Dina, Von, and Jules got into leos, warm-up suits, gym socks, and beam slippers, then gave their hairdos a final blast of extra-hold spray, they observed the impressive teams from the larger schools. Some teams had seven girls in their age group. But they knew that if Flip City's scores were solidly high, the team could make the averages needed to win. Having competed at state level before, the girls all understood the value of consistency, confidence—and a few lucky breaks.

Mercy waved to some girls who were their regular

competitors: the Marvelles, the Flyers, and the Gym-nettes. She then studied the teams from the power-house gyms like US Academy, Gymnastic Universe, and Coliseum Gymnastics. They looked like tough competitors, with impressive warmup suits.

A moment before the warmups were called, a com-manding figure in a Patriots jacket entered the locker room in search of Jules.

"Here we are, Evalene," Jules called.

"Mother got Grandmother settled in the boat seat," Evalene reported to Jules. "So wave at her, O.K. Here is something sent from Father."

Jules opened the long box and discovered lush red American Beauty roses, their stems wrapped in blue and gold ribbons to match Flip City's warmups. Jules read the card:

"Good luck to Flip City's girls, all American Beau-ties. From MacArthur Wolcott."

Eileen told her, "They're super! You can each carry one during the entrance march."

Jules smiled at Evalene. "Daddy remembered, didn't he?"

"He will be out there. Someplace. Don't want to make you nervous. O.K., be strong, be wonderful, my Jewel."

"Bye, Evalene." Jules found Von standing beside her, grinning. "Guess what?" Von said. "I have an-other surprise for you. Which is the boarding school your mother wants you to attend?"

"It's Rosemary Hall. Why?"

"I got a letter yesterday, telling me I won this essay

contest for students with English as a second language. The prize is a free summer—at Rosemary Hall!"

"I can't believe it," Jules said. "That's so wild."

"I'm going this July. We're going to be about fifty kids from all over New England. We'll live in dorms and study English grammar and literature, have parties and picnics."

"Von, I bet you'll have a ball!" Jules gave her a squeeze around the shoulders.

"And I'll tell them Miss Julia is coming soon."

"Maybe not." Jules shrugged with a funny grin. "Looks like all my mid-year grades came up to C level. So Mother is holding back my application. We're having discussions. How about that? Mother and me, discussing!"

"But Jules, I'm going to Rosemary Hall, and you're not?"

Jules laughed. "Mom says it's a fabulous school. But what I need now is Winchester and Flip City. And being home with Mother. When it's time for me to live away at school, I'll know."

"Guess you will," Von agreed. "What about summer for you? Will you spend it with your father?"

"Some of it, at the beach. But what I really want is to go to one of those big gymnastic camps where the handsome Olympians teach. Mother said I could go for July."

"While I'm studying verbs, you'll be studying biceps? Hey, looks like we'll both get what we want!"

"And we'll be back together next fall?"

Von watched the crowd of girls heading for the gym.

"Hope so. If I do really well today, that should help."

Jules also thought about the competition that faced them this afternoon. Although her workouts with Marion had made her feel good about herself, she now felt a sick gnawing at her stomach. She squared her shoulders and followed Von into the noisy gym, glad that Joe was waiting.

Flip City was sent first to warm up on beam. Mercy, Dina, and Loretta joined Von and Jules, doing various stretches, handstands, spins and walkovers on the mat. Dina said to Mercy, "I hope Pop and Rose and Theresa got good seats. The bleachers are all filled up."

As she gazed through the tall decks of bleachers, Dina's gaze froze. Between restless Rose and Theresa sat a very pregnant lady on a pillow. "Oh, no," Dina murmured. "They brought Mom."

Mercy followed Dina's stunned look. "What's the matter? You didn't think she'd miss this one, did you?"

"She's not supposed to come to big meets! It's too tiring. And noisy. And what if I fall? She'll freak out!"

Mercy, already extremely nervous without enduring one of Dina's panic attacks, lost her patience and snapped at her. "Cut it out. You won't get hurt. You're going to win and you know it."

"Yes, but I *could* fall off the beam," Dina continued in a loud whisper. "And what if Mom gets too upset?"

Mercy hissed back, "Eileen and Joe are watching you. Just keep thinking how you'll look standing up there with those gold medals around your neck. Your mom's going to be thrilled."

Dina kept talking in a low choked voice. "I could

pretend I'm sick to my stomach. Mercy, I can't stand
it if anything happens to this baby. You know what I
told you. This baby means everything!"

Mercy leaned close, hoping Eileen was not picking
up a word. "Yes, but what about *you*? You and your
sisters mean everything, Dina. Don't you think she's
proud of the kids she's got? No parent sits through
these meets for *fun*. And what about us? You aren't
the only person here, you know. The team needs you."

Dina shifted her gaze to Mercy's kind sensible face.
"O.K., you're right," she said. "I'm going to stop
worrying. Right now. That's what Mom always tells
me. Don't worry so much. And Mercy . . . last night,
I talked to her a little about Anthony. We just happened to be in my room, by his photo, and I did it."

Dina waited for Mercy's approval. Although she'd
only taken a small step, it had required more emotional
strength than she could have imagined. Who but
Mercy could appreciate that? "That's great," Mercy
smiled. "I know how tough it was . . . because I kind
of did it too. I thought if you had the guts to tell *me*,
then I could do the same with my mother." She looked
at Dina with admiration. Dina was thrilled—but before she could respond, Eileen called to her, "Your
warmup on beam." So Dina only smiled in return, and
went to work. The meet was now, and it was
everything.

By starting time, the Franklin field house was
packed with parents and friends, many holding note-
books and video cameras, ready to record their ath-

lete's attempts at state recognition in her sport. Coaches hustled to line up their teams in the required order for the entrance march. Official team jackets were zipped, flowers held up proudly. A theme from the Olympics blasted over the sound system; twelve teams paraded onto the spring floor for introductions. At the mention of each gym school's name, their fans cheered wildly. The judges were presented, and the meet was opened with the national anthem.

Joe gathered the girls around him at their first event, the vault. "Remember, at a state meet, anyone has a chance to hit it on the money. I've seen a girl score over a 9 on the first routine and never get beaten. I've also seen a girl draw the last slot on floor, when you figure the judges are so tired of that exercise they could choke, and still score a 9.2. The trick is never blow your concentration, because you have a chance to win at any time. Mercy, you're the third vaulter of the day—that can be a great spot. The judges are fresh and eager to see a perfect job. Now all of you, nail it!"

Mercy had avoided looking at her family, who arrived during warmups. The Dibellas had saved them aisle seats so Fred's splints and crutches could stick out. Mercy was afraid that glimpsing Fred struggling to his seat would throw her psyched-up positive frame of mind. She amused herself by watching Von and the Nguyens—mother, father, and two brothers—exchanging looks with the young man seated down front on the bleacher nearest the beam.

"Von," Mercy whispered. "Is that your boyfriend?"

"How could you guess?" Von giggled. "Just because

he's holding a sign that says, 'GO VON! GO FLIP CITY!' "

"That was my first clue. The fact that he's about the cutest hunk here was my second."

Von nibbled the cuticle on her little finger. "He rode his bike all the way out here from the South End."

Mercy winked. "He must be in love."

The girls watched the first two competitors, one from Gymnettes, one from US Academy, take their vaults. Both did well, scoring in the low eights. Mercy realized that at this level, all qualifiers were the best in their schools and were seasoned and experienced. The scores would be tight, with a battle for every tenth of a point.

"You're up, Mercy," Joe said. "Pace it, keep tight, spot your landing."

The girls chanted, "Come on, Mercy, come on, Mercy!" The fervor of their spirit gave Mercy impetus; focused on the horse, she galloped down the runway, paced her final steps, then flew off the springboard. In the few seconds she was airborne, her body movements clicked into position. When she landed, knees bent, arms forward, she rose into a perfect arched salute a fine distance from the horse.

She'd nailed it!

Joe leapt forward and clapped her shoulder. "Super, great form, terrific height. Stick another landing like that and you're in business."

As Mercy trotted back and resumed her stance, she felt positive adrenaline churning, but none of the sick nervous fear she dreaded. So she stuck another one, better than the first. The team screamed with joy. But they had to wait through the next routine to see Mercy's score flashed. Together they watched a US Academy girl take her place. She did not smile or glance at her mates. Her coach waited soberly with arms folded after replacing the board for her. Funny, Mercy thought, how the personality of each coach was different. It showed in how they treated their gymnasts. While some were huggers and kissers after a great exercise, others, like Joe, were more reserved handshakers and shoulder-patters. But some like the US Academy coach seemed to suppress emotion.

The US Academy girl overshot and blew both her landings. Mercy and the Flip City girls stared at the score standard as it was elevated and turned: a 9.05 for Mercy!

"That's the ticket!" Joe shouted. "That's the one to catch!" He clapped Mercy's shoulder, and she fought back the urge to squeal with joy. "Now the rest of you better match her."

Dina gave Mercy's waist a squeeze. "Joe, what happens at awards if there's a tie in scores?"

"At States the competition is so fierce, you can even get three-way ties. The girls stand up together for awards and get identical medals. The judges plan ahead for that."

As Dina nodded, she dreamed of sharing Mercy's first place in vault. If they could stand up together, it would be even better than winning by herself. After several more competitors, Dina rose to take her turn. She sailed confidently over the horse and scored a 9.

While Mercy congratulated her, she grinned. "How about if I stand *next* to you on the platform?"

"Hey, I'm a generous person," Mercy told the team. "You can *all* stand up there with me. Just go for it!"

By the end of the second rotation, during which Flip City shared the bars with the Flyers and Coliseum, competition for points grew intense. Mercy had made it through her bars routine with a 7.8, a generous score. As she sat beside the bars mat, she noticed that most of the gymnasts didn't appear to like the bars much better than she did. After they dismounted and saluted the judges with an obligatory false smile, they stepped off the mat and instantly gave their coaches a look of self-disgust mixed with relief. Most slumped to the mat, and those who wore palm guards tossed them to the floor like refuse. The only one who actually smiled with anticipation was Dina.

Mercy checked out the Dibella and Samuels families. Although the oppressive warmth in the field house made Mrs. Dibella looked flushed and uncomfortable, she kept her eyes glued to Dina as she mounted the bars. Mercy's family also watched eagerly. Ernie sat on the aisle next to Fred, ready to assist him. They shot Mercy a grin. Mercy tried to smile in return, recalling her mother's assurance that they were all "coming back" from Thanksgiving, and that everyone's steps forward were equally important.

Dina soared between the bars, forgetting everything, keeping her mind totally tuned to the position of her body. After springing from the high bar into an amazing arched dismount, she rose on her toes and saluted. She beamed with the pleasure of the experience. The judges grinned in return.

As the team smothered Dina with hugs, she knew this *had* to be the golden moment of her day. But how high could she score? The team had to endure a routine by a Coliseum girl, who also gave a strong, solid performance. But Dina's near-balletic grace could not be matched. The judges awarded her a 9.3, a personal record.

Dina peeked at the family. While Rose and Theresa jumped up and clapped at the score, Mom sat with hands folded across her round tummy, holding her composure. Dina knew Mom was keeping cool for her benefit, for her face was glowing with pride. Pop held up his index finger. Her bars score was so far number one. Could she hold on for the rest of the meet? Only if chance and luck went her way.

The meet directors announced a short break before the last two rotations. "O.K., girls, good show," Joe said. "Get a drink, say hi to the folks. Then get over to the spring floor for our third rotation warmup."

"Grandmother, how're you doing?" Jules asked as she darted to the bleachers for a quick word.

"Just fine, dear," Grandmother replied. "It's so exciting."

"Did you see our bars rotation? Dina's won for sure. But I think I may take fifth or something. Well, maybe not, after US Gymnastics does theirs. But floor's coming up, my best."

"For heaven's sake, Julia," Mother said, the strain showing on her face, "these girls are the best in the

state! We don't expect you to win medals. Just don't
get hurt."

"I won't get hurt, Mother. But I'm going to win a
medal. It's going on a stand by Grandmother's chair
in the den. She knows why." She winked at the lady
in the boat seat.

Grandmother gazed up at Jules, her eyes misty. "It's
the strangest thing, Julia; you look so much older today. Well, go on then, and do it."

Von needed a drink and a dash to the bathroom,
but she still wanted to thank Riccio for making the
long bike ride and bringing the "GO VON!" sign.
When she looked at the far end of the bleacher where
he sat, she could not see him. Confused, she looked
down the deck, then up to where her parents and
brothers sat. Then she grinned. Riccio was "making
his move." He had found a seat only a row down from
them, and was making sure that Von's brothers saw
the sign. Laughing, she pushed her way through the
crowds clogging the aisles along the bleachers until
she stood below them all and waved. That Riccio. He
never gave up. "Just like me," she thought. Then her
nerves got the better of her, and she rushed to the
bathroom.

Dina had decided not to buck the crowds and go
over to speak to her family. Pop was not in his seat
anyway; apparently he'd taken Rose and Theresa outside for a soda. Mom sat alone on her cushion, enduring the shoving fans who climbed over her feet and
the non-stop din that filled the field house. Mom's

eyes met Dina's and she smiled. She set down her knitting and held up her index finger. Number One. Dina nodded.

Mom sat there looking solid as a statue. Somewhere deep within her, Dina realized there was a reservoir of strength and bravery that enabled her to survive the loss of children. And Dina saw for the first time that in one way, the most important way, she and Mom were just alike.

Then she felt very thirsty. So she hurried toward the lobby, where she hoped she could catch Pop and get him to buy her a soda too.

Mercy ran over to Fred and bummed a dollar for a soda. "How are you doing?" she asked. "Not too stiff?"

"Naw, this is fantastic," Fred said. "Competition is incredible. It's going to be so close for you kids."

Mercy's grandparents beamed at her, a new-found admiration in their eyes. Funny, she thought wryly, they hit the one meet where it looks like I'm going to cruise. Plenty of other meets, Mercy recalled, she'd flopped on the vault or fallen off the bars. Sometimes God was very nice to you.

Clutching her dollar, Mercy shoved her way toward the soda table in the foyer. Somehow she managed to get a cola and not have it dumped onto her leo. The only place to stand was against the lit glass trophy cases at the end of the lobby, so Mercy worked her way over to them. To her surprise, she found herself standing next to Marion Rothman who was sipping black coffee.

"Hi, Mercy," Marion smiled. "You're doing a great job today."

"Thanks." Mercy wasn't sure if she was happy to see the old mind-reader.

"I suppose your mother told you I called? Are you put out with me?"

Leave it to Marion to get down to the bottom line, Mercy thought. "I would be—except it turned out O.K."

"Fine. Then we won't ever mention it again. Drink your cola, you only have a few minutes."

As Mercy sipped, her eyes turned to the glass case behind Marion. In a propped frame under bright light stood a huge photo of this year's famed football team, the one that made it to the State Tournament, but didn't quite win, maybe due to the sidelining of the great Fred Samuels . . . who stood center photo, hands on hips, shoulders padded to gorilla size, grinning as he anticipated the season before him, with no splints on his legs. Mercy felt the cola sting her throat.

Marion did it again. Without even turning, she followed the direction of Mercy's gaze and remarked, "Nice picture of your brother. I know it's tough, Mercy, to see him now—but young athletes make remarkable recoveries."

Suddenly, because Marion said it, Mercy believed it *could* be true. But instead of continuing to talk about Fred, Marion changed the subject.

"Are you looking forward to being a student here?"

"Oh, sure; it's a little scary, but sure."

"Lots of sports here," Marion continued. "Not only a gymnastics team, but volleyball, softball; the coaches will be glad to see you. If you want to compete. Have you thought about that, Mercy?"

"Sort of. I guess I'd rather stay in Class III optionals, or try for Class II, along with Dina and Jules and Von. But like my mom says, we can't tell what's coming next in life. I mean, what we can afford and all."

"Hmmm." Marion fixed Mercy with her hazel eyes, then gestured toward the gym. "Better get back to Eileen. Good luck. And *concentrate*."

As she sidestepped through the returning crush and made it to the spring floor, Mercy felt that familiar mixture of annoyance and fascination with Marion. Although Marion's insistence that mental attitude controlled everything bugged Mercy, she had to admit that Marion proved her own point.

Given the difficulty of scoring on a floor exercise that had so many possible slips and mismoves, the girls performed brilliantly as they inspired and drew energy from each other. Mercy scored an 8.3; Dina pulled an 8.4! Von, who then managed an 8, insisted that Dina was tied with two others for first; and Mercy held second. Then the floor gave Jules her personal moment of triumph. As she danced, pranced, leapt and spun, rolled and flipped, Jules felt a confidence she'd never shown before. And with her final splits and pose, she gave them what Marion demanded: *performance*. Her reward came with an 8.6 score.

Eileen gathered the girls around her on the mat as they moved over for the last rotation. "Stay cool and hold your own on beam. It's been a long meet, and the judges know it's tough to do a perfect exercise when you're tired. The scores are edging up a bit, and we'll take advantage of that. Right?"

Mercy and Dina leaned their heads together, and Dina whispered, "You know all that stuff about the beam being lines down a sidewalk? Well, that's only if you're scared. I'm not so scared anymore. It's just a beam. I don't like it—but I can do it."

Mercy nodded. As Von rose to prepare for her turn, Mercy took a look at her family, where Fred and Ernie held the aisle seats and talked animatedly with their grandparents. Beside them, perched on the step, sat Marion. "Von!" Mercy said. "Go for it! Marion's watching. . . ."

Unfortunately, Von had to follow a girl from GU, who performed with such precision and timing that she *had* to get nearly a nine. "Forget her score," Von told herself. "Just flow like the wind." With her every step falling into place, Von sensed that her limbs were following each command with perfect grace. How easy it was sometimes! She took a deep breath, and leapt into a high dismount flip.

Jules hugged her as she returned to the mat. "Fantastico! And just take a look at your fan club."

Von turned as she pulled on her warmups. Riccio was now seated next to her brothers, who cheered and waved the "GO VON!" sign. Mother laughed with relief that her beam went beautifully. Von winked at Jules. "Even if I don't win, I guess we took a step toward world harmony."

Jules chuckled. The next Gymnette finished, and

they all turned for Von's score. Jules shrieked along with the team, then told Von, "A 9.05! Looks like you can have it all!"

Once again in her gym career, Dina found she'd drawn the last slot on the beam. She too had noticed Marion beside the Samuels family, carefully observing her girls. But suddenly she saw a vacant pillow between Rose and Theresa. Mom was gone.

Mercy followed Dina's concerned look. "Oh, hey, I think I saw your mom go out for a drink or something. It's wicked hot."

"Even back in New York," Dina said slowly. "Mom would never watch me work on beam. But I never thought before how it might maybe be her wall too?"

"Maybe," Mercy said. "And she doesn't want to send you any bad vibes. Just go and do it, Dina. That's what she wants."

"It's what I want." Dina rose, shook out her limbs, and approached the beam, which didn't appear as high as usual. As she nodded to Eileen to place her board, Dina pushed them *all* out of her head . . . and conquered the beam alone. Her scale was poised, her handstand solid, her walkover fluid, her dismount perfectly placed. She got an 8.0—a personal best.

Four long hours after they arrived at the State Class III Compulsories, the Flip City group awaited their awards. Stacked mats served as the winners' platform. Some of the exhausted girls flopped on the floor, expressing fits of temper and depression as they complained of being mis-scored. Joe and Eileen would have none of that. "Sit up straight," Joe reminded the

Flip City girls, "and when you're up there, shake hands with your competitors."

But would they all be "up there"? Mercy, Dina, Jules, Von, and Loretta waited intently as awards were announced, starting from the bottom of the top ten in each event. First the winning total scores for personal performance and then overall scores would be announced.

Mercy squeezed Jules's and Dina's hands as the bars scores were called; Jules was delighted with her eighth place medal; but the announcer kept going up without mentioning Flip City until the last name, the first place gold:

"Dina Dibella of Flip City!"

Dina danced onto the winners' platform, pausing to hug Jules on the way up the line, then shook hands with the Coliseum girl standing in second. Although her eyes were misty, she squinted quickly toward the bleachers; Pop and Rose shot their fists in the air with glee, but Mom's head was bowed. Dina rose on her toes to see why—and discovered that she was preoccupied with keeping a sleeping Theresa anchored on her lap. She's proud of *all* her kids, Dina thought, all the kids she's got.

Mercy sweated the call-ups for vault. She'd heard that a US Academy girl had tied her 9.05. As the names were read, the team discovered that Von had pulled eighth, Loretta sixth, and Dina held second; and when Mercy and her competitor walked up to share first place medals, somehow the US Academy girl claimed all the space at the top. So Mercy stood next to Dina, smiled at her friend, and savored the moment.

Von's turn for that trip to the top came with the beam awards; although she shared with a Flyer, her first place medal gave her such a feeling of power and pride, like a talisman around her neck, that Von felt as if she was standing solo on top of the world. And when she peeked at her family, she laughed to see both her brothers and Riccio joined in raucously raising the "boxer's salute" to her! But Von realized that another's medal for beam, although only a ninth place, meant as much as her first—for it went to Dina Dibella, a girl who overcame her fears.

When floor exercise medals were given, Mercy took fifth, Dina fourth, and Jules third. Although the medal wasn't the first-place gold Jules had desired, she still basked in her family's applause.

Eventually, the all-around winners were announced. If every girl from Flip City placed in the top ten, they had a good chance for the Team Trophy. One by one the girls cheered as they each took their place on the platforms: Loretta was tenth, Jules ninth, Mercy tied for sixth, Von tied for fourth—and, only by a half-point, Dina took first. In such a high calibre meet, each girl knew they'd been very lucky indeed.

At last the tabulator stood to announce the team trophy winners. The five nine-to-elevens ran down from the bleachers to gather around Joe and Eileen with the older Threes. Marion leaned against the wall behind the trophy table, letting her younger coaches claim the victory. Finally the announcer reached third.

"We're neck and neck now," he said. "When you coaches get your computer printouts, you'll see what I mean. Third place goes to US Academy. Second place is to Coliseum Gymnastics . . . and first place . . . goes to Flip City!"

When the ten girls stopped screaming and hugging, Joe shoved them as a group toward the platform, where they all held onto the monstrous trophy, indeed a skyscraper with wings. Soon the crowd started to swarm the floor, friends and parents with video cameras whirring and flash cameras popping. Mercy saw Marion raise her hand and point. Even at the best moment of an athlete's life, Mercy was reminded, she must not forget sportsmanship. She put down the trophy and shook hands with the competitors to her left. Then she raised her eyes to meet Marion's again for approval—but Marion had vanished.

After receiving all the locker room congratulations from the Dibellas, Wolcotts, and Nguyens, Mercy grabbed her bag and coat and headed out to the lobby, where her family waited for her. Over her parka the medals hanging around her neck on their red, white, and blue ribbons were displayed: first for vault; fifth for floor; tenth for beam; and sixth all-around. To her surprise, she saw Marion had been talking with her parents. Now what had she done wrong? But when she worked her way over to them, Marion only smiled, shook her hand, said, "Good job, Mercy," and bid her family goodbye.

As they walked out to the parking lot, Mom put her arm around Mercy's shoulders. "Guess what?" she asked. "Marion made us an offer. She said she figures we'll have a tough time next semester with all of Fred's medical bills, and the new car, and so she said if we both come early Saturday mornings, I can do her accounts, and you can help teach the little Class IV girls. And she'll only charge you half tuition. She says its the only deal she ever makes. How about that?"

Mercy stopped, stared with amazement at her mother. "But why me? I may never even make it up to Class II. I'm not that *good*."

"Mercy, what class you make, and how *good* you are, are two different things."

Mercy swallowed the lump of pride rising in her throat. "So what do you think, Mom? It's great with me."

"Things are changing fast for us," Mom said. "Fred'll be leaving for school, probably the State U. Ernie's going to get a job for after school; he wants to earn a good computer. Soon, nobody will be eating those big dinners anymore."

"Yeah, but Mom, there'll still be you and Dad and me. I've got all of high school yet, remember? I'm still a kid!"

"Sometimes we forget that." Mom smiled. "Don't know why."

"Mom, I think we owe it to Marion and old Flip City to keep the place in business. They need us, Mom." The more Mercy spoke, the more she loved the idea. She had to stay at Flip City.

How could the place get along without her?

Glossary of Gymnastic Terms

GENERAL:

Extension: arms, legs, and torso stretched creating a straight line.

Pike: to bend or jackknife the body at the waist, legs straight.

Compulsory: routines required to be performed by all gymnasts in a class, elements prescribed by United States Gymnastics Federation.

Optional: routines which have certain required elements, but with all other moves choreographed individually by the gymnast.

Rotation: time it takes a designated squad in a meet (consisting of girls from several teams) to complete performing on one of the four apparatuses. A squad rotates from vault to bars to beam to floor, but depending on which event the squad draws first, they can begin anywhere in the sequence.

Springboard: an inclined double board with heavy springs sandwiched between layers. It is a piece of equipment used for mounting the beam, the vault, and optionally the bars.

Springfloor: a forty by forty foot wood surface with springs screwed underneath over which flexible foam padding and carpeting are installed.

VAULT: exercises are performed by running for momentum, leaping from a springboard, and then pushing the body off and over the horse, (touching it only with the hands), and striking a posed salute upon landing.

The Handspring Vault: a full front flip pushing high off the horse with the hands, keeping the body in a straight extension and landing forward on both feet solidly, with the horse to the back.

UNEVEN PARALLEL BARS: exercises are performed by swinging from higher to a lower bar of prescribed height and back without the feet touching the ground.

The Kip: gymnast jumps forward and hangs from the bar, swings to an extended position with legs together (the glide), then pikes the legs, pushes down with straight arms to finish the move with front support and bar at hip. In a straddle kip, the legs are straight but separated in scissors position.

The Hip Circle: holding the bar, the gymnast circles the bar 360° with bar at hips.

The Sole Circle: holding the bar, the gymnast circles the bar 360° with bar in instep or sole of the foot.

THE BALANCE BEAM: exercises are performed by mounting the beam, which is four feet off the ground, using either the springboard or free leaps, then performing various acrobatic and dance moves traversing the length of the beam (sixteen feet) for a maximum of one minute fifteen seconds, at which time the gymnast must dismount.

The Scale: a pose or stationary hold, balanced on one foot, in a forward, backward, or sideways position.

The Handstand: a static hold on the hands, with straight body extension.

The Body Wave: a move in which the gymnast balances on both toes and ripples the entire body like a wave.

Leaps: the gymnast takes off on one foot, landing on the other, striving for height and 180° split of the legs.

Walkovers (backward and forward): the gymnast stands with hips squared along the beam, extends back and shoulders into an arch, then places hands back on the beam, passes through a split handstand, keeping legs straight and toes pointed, then finishes in an upright standing pose. The forward walkover is the same move in reverse order.

THE FLOOR EXERCISE: the compulsory routine is performed to a standard tape of music of regulation length, during which time the gymnast may not step out of the boundaries of the spring floor. This routine is composed of different acrobatic and gymnastic elements. Harmony between music and movement is essential. The compulsory components change every four years with the Olympic cycle. All the moves from the balance beam are also performed in floor exercises, with higher difficulty dance moves added.